The Adventures of the Lookout Mountain Gang:
The Secret Chest

By Jill Watson Glassco

Deep Sea Publishing, LLC

Copyright Page

The Adventures of the Lookout Mountain Gang: The Secret Chest, Copyright © 2020 by Jill Watson Glassco

Illustrations: Anya Figert

Cover Design: Ben Glassco

Printed in the USA

ISBN-13: 978-1-939535-39-9
ISBN: 1939535395

www.deepseapublishing.com

TABLE OF CONTENTS

Dedication

For

Rocky, Mark, Freddy, Steve, and Mary

(the best brothers and friends a little girl could have)

and

the good people of Fort Payne, Alabama

Foreword

Lookout Mountain, Fort Payne, Alabama. I left the old neighborhood along its brow forty-six years ago, yet that mountain still swaddles my soul like a homespun quilt—a patchwork of happy, carefree, and untroubled peace. My brother, Rocky, often says, "We were born to the best parents in the best place on earth." I agree.

"Mama," my daughter, Rebecca, said, "you and Uncle Rocky and Uncle Mark have so many stories. You should write a book about your childhood."

So, I did. In most ways, *The Adventures of the Lookout Mountain Gang: The Secret Chest* is a real-name-real-place autobiography through my eyes as a seven-year-old in 1963. Because every good story needs a captivating plot, however, imagination (stoked by Rebecca, my granddaughter Anya, and a childhood friend and neighbor, Freddy Eberhart) is woven into sweet memories and hometown history. (Freddy, I hope this story brings a smile in heaven.)

"For the joy of human love,

Brother, sister, parent, child,

Friends on earth, and friends above,

For all gentle thoughts and mild;

Christ our God, to Thee we raise,

This our hymn of grateful praise."[1]

_____

[1] FOR THE BEAUTY OF THE EARTH. Lyrics: Folliott Sandford

Pierpont, 1864. Melody: DIX, Conrad Kocher, 1838.

Chapter 1:

A Secret

"For all that is secret will eventually be brought into the open, and everything that is concealed will be brought to light and made known to all." (Luke 8:17 NLT)

"But we don't love her like you do, Mark. Why does *she* always have to tag along?" Freddy complained.

"Yeah," Steve, Freddy's younger brother, chimed in. "Why does Jill-dill-pickle have to go?"

I scrunched my freckled face to hide the welling tears and stuck out my tongue at the neighbor boys. In my mind, I was one of the gang, not an unwelcome guest.

Mark reached for my hand. (Since the day Mama and Daddy brought me home from the DeKalb County Hospital in 1956, my big brother by two and a half years had been my guardian angel. I used to think that every kid had a mama, a daddy, and a Mark.)

"Aw, she's not hurtin' nothin'," he said. "Besides, there aren't any little girls for her to play with in the neighborhood."

Five small houses under a thicket of trees made up our neighborhood, which stretched down a gravel road along the lower brow of Lookout Mountain. Earlier that summer, the Public Works Department had covered the dry-dust potholes and rainy-day mud with crushed Fort Payne chert, a light-olive-gray limestone blasted from the mountainside at the hometown quarry. The hard, sharp rocks leveled the road for cars alright, but made for many a bloody knee in bicycle wrecks.

We followed a trail into the woods to a pine-bough teepee. Fresh cut evergreens perfumed the warm June air.

Yesterday, Mark (who would turn ten before school started back in the fall) had chopped down pine saplings with his new hatchet and stripped the limbs. Freddy, Steve, and I helped him lean the bare trunks against a tall hickory. We covered the wood frame with thick-needled branches, leaving a gap in the front for the doorway.

At the hut, Steve set a rusty bucket on the ground. Buttercup bulbs "borrowed" from Grandmother Eberhart's flowerbed filled it to the brim.

~

Grandmother Eberhart's flowerbed sat beside house number one in the neighborhood where Freddy and Steve's grandparents, Aunt Evelyn, and Uncle Norman lived. It had two kitchens—a small one for everyday cooking and a spacious one for canning vegetables in the summertime and making the best popcorn balls and candied apples in the state of Alabama at Halloween.

Ten-year-old Freddy and nine-year-old Steve Eberhart lived in house number two with their parents, two dogs, Snowball and Willie Bo Jokin', and Wilbur Sifter—a little stuffed monkey that held a place of prominence on Steve's bookshelf.

The Fred Raymond family lived in house number three with one teenage daughter and two mean collies, Prissy and Teakie, that barked, growled, and showed their vicious teeth when anybody passed by. Oftentimes, the kids in the neighborhood cut through the woods to avoid their grumpy dogs.

Mark and I lived in house number four with our parents, Winfred and Verna Watson, and our older brother, Rocky. Rocky was almost fourteen and liked to spend his summer days playing baseball with friends at an empty corner lot on Forest Avenue near our grandparents' house down in the valley between Lookout Mountain and Sand Mountain. But the second week of summer vacation, his life changed big-time. Daddy woke him up at the crack of dawn one morning and announced that Rocky had a new job, working for him as an abstractor (somebody who sits at the courthouse all day checking title history on real estate property). Daddy said, "Boy, you'll never go hungry if you know how to abstract."

Two hunting dogs, Sue (the best pointer in DeKalb County) and Rip, also lived at our house along with Mama Cat, a black and orange stray that showed up one rainy Halloween night. After that night, a bunch of kittens showed up at house number four a couple times each year. (Last summer, Mama Cat "married" a wild lynx from the woods. One kitten from the litter, Blue Boy, had a bobbed tail.)

Past the first four houses, the road crooked and twisted for about a mile along the rocky bluff until it dead-ended at house number five where the Winters family lived with five teenagers and no telephone. (My family shared a party-line with the Eberharts and the Raymonds.)

Because city water had yet to make it up the mountain, each house in the neighborhood had its own well. Daddy was really good at building stuff and fixing things, so he rigged a red light on our well house to signal low-water levels. Nobody dared flush the one toilet, take a "navy" shower, or even turn on a faucet when the light was on, which happened practically every day. Rocky had spent every birthday wish since he was two years old hoping for ample water.

~

Freddy dug in the dirt with his fingers and dropped an onion-shaped bulb into the hole. He wiped grimy hands on his shorts and announced, "We gotta secret."

"What's the secret?" Mark asked.

"Can't tell," Freddy said smugly.

I frowned. "Then why'd ya tell us you got a secret?"

"Is it a new puppy?" Mark asked.

"Nope," Freddy and Steve said together.

"Kitty?" I guessed.

"Nope. You'll *never* guess."

"I'll let you use my new hatchet if you tell us the secret," Mark wheedled.

Steve eyed the small, shiny axe strapped into a leather holster on Mark's belt. "Well, you can't tell anybody. Promise?" he said. "Cross your heart and hope to die?"

"I promise," Mark said.

"Wait a minute," Freddy objected. "What about *her*? She's a little blabbermouth."

"I won't tell," I promised, then crossed my heart with my finger.

"Here." Freddy shoved the bucket of bulbs into my skinny arms. "You plant the rest of these, and we *might* tell you the secret."

The red sun had dropped under Sand Mountain by the time I finished digging and planting, digging and planting, and digging and planting. My knees hurt. My legs itched, and black dirt covered both hands and up to my elbows.

In the twilight, the boys hauled a bucket of water from Granddaddy Eberhart's fishing pond on the other side of the woods and watered the promise-of-a-garden. Bullfrogs bellowed from the cattails. Lightning bugs winked on and off, on and off over the woods, and a symphony of crickets and katydids sang to the rising moon. Suddenly, the CLANG, CLANG, CLANG of a brass hand bell sounded from the front porch of house number four.

"Come on, Jill. We gotta go. Mama's callin'," Mark said and started down the path. "See y'all tomorrow."

"Wait a minute," I hollered and stomped my foot. "I planted *all* those flowers, and I'm not budgin' till they tell me that secret."

Out of the growing darkness, a dog howled in the distance.

Freddy murmured, "Ooo, maybe it's the *wendigo*."

My eyes grew to two brown saucers. "Wait, Mark! I'm comin'," I cried and ran like the wendigo was on my heels.

"The Wendigo" was a scary television tale set in the Canadian northwest about hunters tracking down a creepy beast that snatched up people and toted them off. Walter Matthau was one of the stars. The first episode had given me nightmares for a week, so our folks never let us watch it again.

Freddy laughed.

"Let's tell 'em," Steve whispered. "Maybe they can help us figure it out."

Freddy nodded. "Okay, right after swimming lessons tomorrow."

REFLECTIONS

A POINT TO PONDER

When Freddy complained about me tagging along, how did I feel?

A PEARL FROM GOD

"The LORD will not reject His people; He will not abandon His special possession." (Psalm 94:14 NLT)

A PRINCIPLE TO LIVE BY

You always have a faithful Friend in Jesus. Imitate Him. Be a faithful friend to others, treating them the way you want to be treated.

Chapter 2:

Little Fishes

"...fish...that swim the paths of the seas."

(Psalm 8:8 NIV)

Because Mama hadn't learned to swim until the spring of 1940 as a freshman at the University of Alabama, she was bound and determined that all of us kids would swim like fish in the sea. Every summer, like clockwork, two weeks of mandatory swimming lessons always followed the week of Vacation Bible School.

Daddy cranked open the windows of his white and mint-green 1960 Willis jeep, and Mark and I scrambled into the back seat. We stopped at the corner where the chert road made a ninety-degree turn between house number two and house number three and picked up Freddy and Steve. They smelled like Coppertone suntan lotion. Daddy shifted the gearstick to first, and we chugged down the mountain to the city pool.

In the cool of the morning, the large, unheated pool felt like chlorinated ice water. Beginners splashed in the shallow end, intermediate swimmers leaped from two diving boards in the middle, and the more advanced swimmers trained in the deep end under the spine-tingling high dive. Somehow, I'd managed to weasel my way into the top group with Mark, Freddy, and Steve. In my mind, wherever those boys were, that's where I belonged.

~

In the spring, I'd talked Mama and Daddy into letting me join the boys in the church confirmation class fashioned for nine to twelve-year-olds. Because the homework assignments were too hard for a first grader, Mama had read them out loud and helped me print the fill-in-the-blank answers.

The day after my seventh birthday (Palm Sunday, April 7, 1963), when the class stood before the Methodist congregation, Mama heard a whisper behind her, "Who's that little one in the front row?"

~

Today's swimming lesson began with a ten-minute warm-up: treading water for five minutes and then paddling in a circle like a raft of ducks until Bobby, the instructor, blew a whistle and hollered, "Okay, kids, practice your strokes: American crawl first, then breaststroke, backstroke, and sidestroke. Get moving."

We splashed around the deep end for two hours. (Well, maybe not that long, but it sure seemed like it.) Bobby finally blew the whistle and yelled, "Line up at the high dive."

I slipped to the back of the line. High places give me the heebie-jeebies, and I hated the high dive. Daddy said that people who are afraid of heights are called acrobats. No, wait a minute; that's not right. Hydrophobics? Acrophobics? Well, some kind of phobics. Anyhow, I reckon I must be one 'cause the butterflies in my stomach danced a hoedown, and my legs felt like wet noodles as I crawled up the ladder behind the other kids.

Step by s-l-o-w step, I inched my way to the end of the board towering above the ice-blue water. Looking down, down, down, I felt like a skydiver about to jump out of an airplane without a parachute. My feet stuck to the board like glue.

"You're okay," Bobby called. "I'm coming. Don't move, Jill."

Don't worry; I'm NOT movin', I thought.

He walked out to me and said, "Squat down and put your hands on the end of the board."

I clutched the diving board so tightly that my knuckles went white. Bobby picked me up by the heels. The other kids in the class clung to the side of the pool. All eyes focused on upside-down me.

"Ready?" he said.

No! I thought. "Yes, sir," I squeaked.

"On three. One, two, three!" he said and then dropped me into the water.

SPLAT!

The perfect belly buster plus embarrassment turned my face as red as a lobster. Mark swam toward me.

"You okay?" he asked.

I forced a laugh but wanted to cry. "Yeah, I'm fine," I lied.

From the platform, Bobby blew the final whistle, ending our last swimming lesson for the summer. Freddy, Steve, Mark, and I scrambled from the chilly water. We wrapped in beach towels and flip-flopped toward the jeep waiting in the gravel parking lot.

"Tell 'em," Steve whispered.

"Not yet," Freddy said.

REFLECTIONS

A POINT TO PONDER

How did I feel at the top of the high dive? What are you afraid of?

A PEARL FROM GOD

"But when I am afraid, I will put my trust in You."
(Psalm 56:3 NLT)

A PRINCIPLE TO LIVE BY

When you are afraid, stop thinking about yourself and your circumstances and focus on God, who is great and awesome. Trust the One who is willing and able to help you in everything.

Chapter 3:

Handwriting on the Wall

"Stand at the crossroads and look; ask for the ancient paths, ask where the good way is and walk in it, and you will find rest for your souls." (Jeremiah 6:16 NIV)

Inside the jeep, Mark said, "Guess where we went last Saturday."

"Where?" Steve asked.

"Manitou Cave," I chirped.

Disappointment painted Mark's face. "Ah, Jill, I was gonna tell 'em," he said.

"Sorry," I muttered.

"Well, anyway, Walter was our guide, and he let me hold the flashlight," Mark said. "And I found a bat hanging from the ceiling of the cave."

~

A few blocks south of the city pool, Manitou Cave tunnels a mile deep into the heart of Lookout Mountain. Since 1903, Mr. Raymond's family of house number three in the neighborhood had owned the property. In 1961, after ten years of renovation— replacing rickety wooden steps and slippery bridges with concrete and steel, copper-wiring the cave with electricity, and building a Visitors Center and Gift Shop—the Raymonds reopened the cave for guided tours, and families from the neighborhood got in free.

~

"Manitou Cave has quite a history," Daddy said. "Do you kids know its story?"

I shrugged. "Mr. Walter told us a bunch of stuff on Saturday, but I don't remember what he said."

"Well, Manitou is an Ojibwa word that means *spirit,* but the cave's past is actually tied to the Cherokee Nation. In the early 1800s, a Cherokee scholar named Sequoyah invented a written language for his people called syllabary."

"What's silly berry?" I asked.

Daddy laughed, which made his shoulders jump up and down, which made me laugh, too.

"*SYL-LA-BA-RY* are characters that represent syllables instead of single letters like our ABCs," he explained. "Do you remember those black marks on the rock walls and ceiling?"

"Yes, sir," Mark said.

"Well, those markings are Cherokee syllabary. The old folks around here claim that Sequoyah's moccasins once tread the same underground clay pathways we walked last Saturday. As a matter of fact, in a deeper part of the cave not opened to tourists, the signature of Sequoyah's son was found."

Steve's jaw dropped. "Really?"

"Yes, really, and what's even more fascinating to me is the messages overhead were written backwards."

"Why?" I asked.

"Because those marks are prayers to God," Daddy said. "The Cherokee people wrote them backwards so that God could read their prayers from heaven above."

"How'd they get way up there?" I asked. "It's really high."

"Good question," Daddy said. "I don't know."

"I wish I could read Cherokee syllabary," Mark said.

I nodded. "Me, too."

"Later on, during the Civil War, the cave was mined for saltpeter," Daddy continued, "and by the 1880s, it was opened as a tourist attraction by the Fort Payne Coal and Iron Company. Remember the ballroom?"

"That's where Walter turned off all the lights and made it so dark that I couldn't even see my hand in front of my face," I said.

"That's right. Well, the coal company held social events in the ballroom back in those days, and folks danced to a thousand candle lights."

"Rocky said if you dug a tunnel from the ballroom straight up to the top of the mountain, you'd come out in our living room," I said. "Is that really true?"

Daddy's shoulders shook again as he chuckled. "Well, I don't know about that, sugar. Freddy and Steve, have y'all been in the cave?"

"We've been there three times already," Freddy bragged.

I puffed up like a blowfish. "Well, we've been in Manitou Cave so many times I've lost count!"

Daddy's eyes met mine in the rearview mirror. I hushed. Like him, I could argue with a fence post. I don't really mean to quarrel; I just figure a bigger story might make me a shining star in the boys' eyes.

Daddy stopped the jeep at the corner of the neighborhood. As Freddy and Steve climbed out, Mark asked, "Can y'all play this afternoon?"

Freddy bent down and whispered, "Meet us at the tee-pee for a secret council meeting right after lunch."

REFLECTIONS

A POINT TO PONDER

I thought a bigger story would make me more popular. Did my notion align with God's ways or the world's way of thinking?

A PEARL FROM GOD

"God opposes the proud but gives grace to the humble. So, humble yourself before God...Come close to God, and God will come close to you." (James 4:6-8 NLT)

A PRINCIPLE TO LIVE BY

Humility is not thinking less of yourself; it's thinking of yourself less and thinking of others more—their needs and their feelings.

Chapter 4:

Buried Treasure

"...and the treasures of the town were not destroyed..."
(Joshua 8:27 NLT)

Inside the pine hut, we sat in a cross-legged circle. Outside, a blue jay scolded its bushy-tailed archrival—a squirrel chattering on a neighboring oak branch.

~

In the summertime, folks around town paid no mind to the big-eyed, acorn-eating critters scampering through the woods and around the backyards, but in the fall, two squirrels would be the talk of the town. Every September, Mr. Houston, at Southern Hardware on Gault Avenue, decorated his store window with colorful leaves, bare branches, and two *live* squirrels.

Mr. Houston was a kind man with three boys of his own. One Easter, when the "Easter Bunny" brought Mark a beany-copter hat from Southern Hardware, the propeller was missing. Just one quick phone call sent the storekeeper scurrying back to his shop (even though it was Sunday and a holiday to boot). Mr. Houston found the missing piece and saved the day.

~

Freddy puffed his granddaddy's empty smoking pipe and solemnly passed it to Mark. Mark puffed air and passed to Steve. After Steve took a deep puff, I reached for the pipe.

Freddy held up his hand. "No maidens allowed in the sacred pipe ceremony, only braves. The World Book Encyclopedia says so."

"I'm brave," I said and snatched the pipe from Steve.

Freddy rolled his eyes, "Okay, then, repeat after me: I cross my heart and hope to die."

Mark and I echoed, "I cross my heart and hope to die."

"And stick a needle in my eye," Freddy said.

"Ooo, yuck!" I groaned.

"Say it, or I won't tell you the secret," Freddy declared.

"Okay. And stick a needle in my eye," I mumbled.

"If I tell anybody the sacred Eberhart secret," Freddy said.

"If I tell anybody the sacred Eberhart secret," we vowed.

"Now, say, 'I promise' and spit on the ground," Freddy said.

"I promise," Mark said. Ptooey!

"I promise, too," I said. Ptooey. Spittle dribbled down my chin.

"Okay, good. Well, a long, long, long time ago, way back in 1887," Freddy began, "Fort Payne was just a sleepy, little town sittin' in the middle of an Alabama cotton patch."

I hugged my knees and leaned in.

"All peaceful and quiet, that is, until a fellow heard about folks getting rich quick in the mineral mines down in Birmingham and Bessemer. He wanted in on the big bucks, too, so the man started a rumor. He claimed that our town had buried treasure—rich deposits of iron and coal that would make everybody millionaires or maybe even billionaires!"

Our wide eyes focused on Freddy, the master storyteller.

"Before you could say Yankee Doodle went to town, folks from up north came a rushing down to Fort Payne like chickens on a June bug, hopin' to find their fortune. And the story's told that four sharp-as-a-tack business men fueled the fortune-hunting fire. They raised five *million* dollars and started the Fort Payne Coal and Iron Company."

"Five million dollars! How'd they do that?" I asked.

"They sold fifty thousand shares of stock at a hundred dollars a share," Freddy said.

"Hey, the Fort Payne Coal and Iron Company—that's the one Daddy told us about that held those dances back in the ballroom of Manitou Cave," Mark said.

"One and the same," Freddy agreed. "Well, anyhow, everybody got so excited about getting rich that the whole town exploded. That's why they called it the *Boom* Days. New stores and buildings and mines started poppin' up everywhere like surprise lilies on a fall day."

"The Iron and Coal Company even built an Opera House. It's still standing on Gault Avenue just down the street from Grandmother Kellett's house. And they built a humongous, fancy hotel called the DeKalb Hotel. It was three stories tall and had over 100 luxurious rooms and a ballroom with really expensive gold and crystal chandeliers and a billiard room, too."

"What's a billiard room?" I asked.

"A room with pool tables," Steve said.

"You mean like that nasty old pool hall down on First Street?" I asked. "Mama says that's a bad place. One time, me and Sharon walked by and stuck our heads in the door. A raggedy, old man with a cigarette hanging out of his mouth told us to git."

"What'd you do?" Steve asked.

"We ran like Mama Cat when the dogs chase her up a tree," I said.

Steve laughed.

"Well, the DeKalb Hotel's billiard room was *nothing* like the pool hall. It was all shiny and clean and fancy like a palace," Freddy said. "Everything the Iron and Coal Company built was elegant and fine as china. They even made a park across the street from the hotel and named it Union Park to make the Yankees feel more at home."

"This sure is a *long* secret," I muttered.

"Shhh," Mark said, hanging on every word. "Go on, Freddy."

"But, sadly to say, in just three short years, the small pockets of iron and coal petered out. So, as fast as folks rushed into town, they started rushin' out. Well, there was this one very, very old, really, really rich lady that had moved to town from Boston, and before she left Fort Payne, she sent her carriage driver to the DeKalb Hotel with a heavy chest of drawers strapped to the back of a wagon."

"The driver went straight to the hotel manager and delivered an important message: 'This valuable chest came all the way from Germany, and madam insists on giving it to the city of Fort Payne. She said that its beauty goes beyond the seen, and you must search for the unseen beauty.' Then the man walked out the door, and nobody ever saw him or the very, very old, really, really rich lady ever again."

"It took four strong men to carry the chest inside. Ornate carvings decorated the beautiful curved-walnut chest, and royal-blue felt lined the drawers. On the top, three polished-bronze knights dressed in shining armor and riding on horseback sat battle ready. The chest stayed on display in that magnificent hotel's lobby until one bitter-cold February night in 1918. On that dark, fateful night..."

"What does fateful mean?" I asked.

Mark shushed me again and nodded for Freddy to keep going.

"On that fateful night, the DeKalb Hotel caught fire and *burned* to ashes. Only one solitary piece of furniture survived." Freddy paused dramatically. "The chest of drawers," he whispered.

"The chest of drawers?" I yelled. "That's the secret? That's the dumbest secret I've ever heard. You made me cross my heart and hope to die and spit for that? That's not a good secret."

"I'm not finished!" Freddy cried.

Steve blurted out, "It's in Grandmother Eberhart's attic! We found the chest of drawers last Saturday, and Grandmother said nobody ever found the unseen beauty. So, me and Freddy, we're gonna find it."

"No, it's not. You're just making that up," I said.

"Am not," Freddy said.

"Are to," I argued.

"I'll prove it. We'll show you," Freddy said.

"Let's go!" Mark said.

REFLECTIONS

A POINT TO PONDER

In the beanie-cap story, did Mr. Houston act selfishly or selflessly?

A PEARL FROM GOD

"Don't be selfish; don't try to impress others. Don't look out for your own interests, but take an interest in others, too. You must have the same attitude that Christ Jesus had. Though He was God, He did not think of equality with God as something to cling to. Instead, He gave up His divine privileges; took the humble position of a slave and was born as a human being. When He appeared in human form, He humbled Himself in obedience to God and died a criminal's death on a cross. Therefore, God elevated Him to the place of highest honor and gave Him the name above all other names!" *(Philippians 2:3-9 NLT)*

A PRINCIPLE TO LIVE BY

Self*ish*ness never wins friends. Self*less*ness or the concern for others over oneself, however, builds good friendships, strong communities, and a better world. Let's live selflessly.

Chapter 5:

Old and Forgotten

"...Forgetting the past and looking forward to what lies ahead." (Philippians 3:13 NLT)

Freddy, Steve, Mark and I climbed the dropdown ladder in house number one of the neighborhood and shined our flashlights around the dark, musty attic. Cobwebs hung from the open rafters, and rough planks covered the floor. On one side of the trapdoor, an army duffle bag from World War II leaned against a footlocker with a broken hinge. A cane-bottomed rocker with a gaping hole in the woven strips sat on the other side. Mark said that the old and forgotten keepsakes made him feel lonesome and kind of homesick. Not me. Mice and spiders and bugs were all I could think about.

"Over here," Steve said.

He zigzagged between a worn suitcase and a stack of cardboard boxes marked "photos 1920s," "photos 1930s," and "photos 1940s" and shined his Eveready-Captain light into the far corner. The bright beam found a dusty chest of drawers topped with three tarnished-green knights.

I couldn't believe my eyes. "It *is* true!"

Freddy grinned. "Told ya so."

"Can we look for the secret, too?" Mark asked.

We searched every inch of the chest from top to bottom and side to side. Freddy opened every drawer and ran his fingers into the corners, over the moth-eaten felt, and behind the back panels but found nothing that would pass muster as "unseen beauty."

"Scoot it out; let's check the back," Mark suggested.

Nothing. Sweat dripped from our red faces.

"I'm hot," I complained. "Let's go."

Mark studied the sturdy curved legs. "Wait a minute," he said. "We didn't look under it."

"I'm not putting my hand under there," I said. "There's probably a-bajillion spiders."

Steve grabbed an old, wooden tennis racket with Spalding printed on the handle and got down on all fours. He shoved it under the chest and swept back and forth. Cobwebs wrapped the racket like cotton candy. A tiny spider scurried out from underneath.

"See. Told ya so," I said.

"Shine the light under there and see if you see anything," Mark said.

"Nope," Steve answered, "just more spider webs and a dead roach."

"Come on. Let's go get popsicles," I said. "Mama made grape ones last night."

REFLECTIONS

A POINT TO PONDER

Did I believe Freddy's story about the old chest of drawers? Did my attitude encourage Freddy and build him up?

A PEARL FROM GOD

"So, encourage each other and build each other up…" (1 Thessalonians 5:11 NLT)

A PRINCIPLE TO LIVE BY

Resolve to be a trusting friend—one who is loving, kind, and encouraging in thoughts, words, and actions.

Chapter 6:

Look It Up

"Look straight ahead and fix your eyes on what lies
before you." (Proverbs 4:25 NLT)

Mama ran tap water over the molds to loosen the frozen grape juice. Ever since the "snowball" incident back in June of '59, she made sure that icy treats were always on hand in the Frigidaire.

~

I was three years old at the time. Mark five. Rocky nine. Mama had promised us 10¢ snowballs from the soda fountain at the Fort Payne Drugstore if we didn't kill each other at the A&P. But when we got to the corner of Gault Avenue and First Street, she couldn't find a parking spot. So, that woman drove right on up the mountain empty-handed—no crushed ice drenched in sugary fruit-flavored syrup in paper cones. I got as mad as a hornet.

At home, Rocky and Mark got tired of my wailing and came up with a *brilliant* plan: sneak me a dime and help me out the back window. "Now, go get your own snowball," Mark said.

After I was well on my way down the chert road in the neighborhood, Rocky reconsidered. "You know, it probably wasn't a good idea for her to go by herself." So, my *dear* brothers tattled, "Uh, Mama, Jill ran away to go get a snowball."

Mama hopped in the car and caught me before I reached the busy highway. I got a spanking. Mark and Rocky didn't. (It would be years before they confessed as my partners in crime.)

~

Mama handed out the homemade popsicles and said, "Your faces are all as red as beets. What have you been up to?"

I piped, "We were up in Grandmother Eberhart's…"

Mark elbowed "chatty-Cathy" me.

"Uh…just playin' at Grandmother Eberhart's house. Whew, it's hot today," I sputtered and stuffed my mouth with the purple pop.

"Mama, will you make a pie if we pick enough blackberries this afternoon?" Mark asked, quickly changing the subject.

"Yes, sugar, but y'all put on long pants and long-sleeved shirts so the briars don't scratch you," she said. "And watch for snakes."

"Yes, ma'am," we promised.

The best blackberry patch in the neighborhood grew over the dam of Granddaddy Eberhart's fishing pond. Past the dam, the spillway fueled a small creek that snaked through the woods, tunneled under the chert road, and eventually dropped over the edge of the mountain. In the wintertime, the waterfall froze into long, sparkly icicles.

~

One cold afternoon two winters prior, Mark was standing near the falls throwing rocks over the ledge. Freddy, Steve, and I decided to sneak along the bluff below him, work our way around to the other side, and then could jump out and scare him. Our plan ran right on track until Mark chucked a fist-sized stone toward the valley and...

BONK!

The rock conked me right on top of the head, leaving a one-inch gash. I started bawling like Mama Cat in a rainstorm.

Mark scrambled down the hill, picked me up, carried me all the way to house number four, dropped me at the back door, and ran inside yelling, "Whip me, Mama! Whip me!"

In the meantime, Rocky heard all the commotion and opened the door to a blood-soaked me. Then, he started yelling, "Mama! Mama! Come here, quick!"

That afternoon was one of the few times in my childhood that I can remember Mama calling for reinforcements. Daddy sped home to stay with my distraught brothers. Mama drove me to Dr. Igou's office for stitches, and Freddy and Steve crept up the road to house number one, looking as white as ghosts. Grandmother Eberhart said they sank down on her couch and didn't say a word.

~

In the blazing sun, bumblebees and iridescent June bugs buzzed about our heads as we picked the plump, dark berries and dropped them into metal buckets. I sang:

> *"I'm taking home a baby bumblebee,*
>
> *Won't my mama be so proud of me.*

I'm taking home a baby bumblebee.

OUCH!

He bit me!"

"Freddy, do you really think there's something hidden in that old chest of drawers?" Mark asked and popped a bittersweet berry into his mouth.

Freddy swatted a fly. "Grandmother believes there is," he said.

Berry picking sounds like fun until you're actually baking in the sweltering sun and fighting stickers and gnats and mosquitoes and flies. After I'd had all the "fun" I could stand for one afternoon, I moaned, "Do we have enough berries yet? I'm burning up."

Mark looked from bucket to bucket. "Not yet. Keep pickin'. It's like a real mystery. Now, what did that rich, old lady say again?"

"She said that the beauty of the chest went beyond what they could see, and they had to look for the unseen beauty," Freddy said.

"Aren't y'all hot?" I asked.

Mark cocked his head to one side, ignoring me. "Unseen beauty? What in the world could that mean?"

"Ask Mama," I said.

"We can't. It's a secret," Mark said. "Besides, you know what she'll say."

"Look it up," we spouted at the same time.

~

Having earned a Bachelor of Library Science at the University of Alabama and worked as a librarian for the armed forces special services at Camp Anza, Los Angeles, Port of Embarkation while Daddy was stationed at Camp Haan during World War II, our Mama was a crackerjack wordsmith. When anyone of us kids asked the meaning of a word or how to spell it, she pointed to Mr. Webster and the encyclopedias, smiled her sweet smile, and said, "Look it up." I always wondered how anybody could look up a word they didn't know how to spell.

~

"Hey, maybe we *should* look it up," Freddy said.

"What would we look for?" Steve asked.

"I don't know. Maybe old chest of drawers or old furniture with hidden beauty?" Freddy said.

I stared at the sprinkle of berries over the bottom my pail. "Do we have enough yet? I'm melting!"

"Almost," Mark said. "Mama's blackberry pie is my favorite. I can taste it now." He licked his lips. "Mmm."

"Mama's double-crust lemon pie is my favorite," I said.

"I like chocolate cake," Freddy said.

"I like any kind of cake that anybody makes," Steve said, "and pies, too."

Freddy, Steve, and I emptied our buckets into Mark's.

"Your mama said we only need two or three cups," Steve said. "This looks like enough to me. Come on; let's go."

"Yay!" I cheered.

We trotted down the worn path across the dam, along the pond, and into the woods. At the pine-bough tee-pee, I stopped to check the flower garden.

"Nothing yet," I said.

"Silly dill pickle," Steve said. "We just planted 'em yesterday."

At house number four, we set the berries on the kitchen counter and jumped down two steps into the playroom—originally, the one-car garage. Brown tile now covered the cement floor and a light fixture made from an old wagon wheel hung from the board ceiling. Two heavy sliding doors stretched across the far wall, concealing packed storage space and a Sears-and-

Roebuck washing machine. (Wire strung between two poles outside served as the clothes dryer).

Beside the sliding doors was a closet that had housed our first well. When that well went dry, our good neighbor, Mr. Eberhart, let Daddy dig a new one on his land across the road between the oil-drum garbage cans and the new piney tee-pee. For safety, a heavy millstone capped the dry well in the closet now crowded with balls, bats, gloves, a toy barn, and a cardboard box filled with farm animals, horses, wagons, cowboys, Indians, and green plastic soldiers.

Bookshelves lined the near wall. Freddy pulled the "C" volume of the 1960 World Books from the shelf and looked up "chest of drawers." Mark pulled the "F" volume and looked up "furniture."

"Find anything?" Steve asked.

"Not yet," Freddy said.

Mark scanned the page and found *Antique Furniture*. "Hey! Listen to this." He read excitedly,

"Nineteenth-century furniture sometimes contained secret compartments for hiding valuable possessions. Woodworkers created false bottoms, secret drawers, or concealed panels where hidden treasures such as valuable jewelry, money, letters, journals, deeds, and even handwritten confessions have been found."

REFLECTIONS

A POINT TO PONDER

Why do you think our mother told us to look things up instead of telling us the answers?

A PEARL FROM GOD

"Work hard and become a leader; be lazy and become a slave." (Proverbs 12:24 NLT)

A PRINCIPLE TO LIVE BY

Don't expect others to do the work for you. Work hard and don't be lazy. God tells us to work as though we are working for Him rather than people (Read Colossians 3:23).

Chapter 7:

Imagine

"No eye has seen, no ear has heard, no mind has imagined what God has prepared for those who love Him." (1 Corinthians 2:9 NLT)

Freddy and Steve stayed for supper. After meatloaf, black-eyed peas, cornbread, and homemade macaroni and cheese made from left over spaghetti noodles, we gobbled down two bowls each of the delicious deep-dish blackberry cobbler and guzzled tall glasses of half-and-half milk—half Carnation dry milk (to save money because our family drank fourteen gallons a week when school was out in the summertime) and half homogenized milk delivered to our doorstep weekly by the Pet milkman. (At Christmastime, the milkman and the paper-lady, who delivered the early morning edition of the Birmingham News, would each get one of Mama's famous orange-glazed pound cakes, and she'd bake a third one to take to Christmas dinner at Granddaddy and Grandmama Nance's house.)

After supper, we played "ain't no boogers out tonight" and chased lightning bugs until Mrs. Eberhart called Freddy and Steve home at bedtime.

When house number four was dark and quiet, I tip-toed down the hall and found Mark staring at the plywood board under the top bunk where Rocky was sleeping like a log.

"You awake?" I whispered.

"Yeah," Mark answered.

I sat down on the edge of the bottom bunk. Night sounds drifted through the open windows. A breeze set the birds on the homemade cotton curtains to flight, and moon-shadows danced over the hardwood floor. His crisp sheets and pillowcase smelled of All detergent and Niagara clothes starch.

"I can't sleep," I whispered.

"Me neither," Mark said and closed his eyes.

"Whatcha doin'?" I asked.

"Imaginin'," he answered.

~

Mama and Daddy declared that Mark was born with an overactive imagination. Even as a little tot, they often found him jumping around a dark living room in the middle of the night on some fanciful adventure. One night, he let out a blood-curdling scream. When Mama and Daddy rushed to see what was wrong, he said, "I was imagining opening the closet door and seeing monsters. One was so scary, I yelled."

In church, if Mark closed his eyes and started fidgeting, Mama would grab his hands and hold them still. "So, people won't think there's something wrong with him," she said.

~

"Whatcha imaginin'?" I asked.

"I just opened a secret drawer in the old chest," he said, "and found hundreds and hundreds of one-hundred-dollar-bills."

"Wow! Then what happened?" I asked.

"I gave the hidden treasure back to the city of Fort Payne, and the high school wildcat band played 'God Bless America,' and Albert Owens, the Chief of Police, hung a shiny medal on a red ribbon around my neck. Then Sheriff Richards and Officer Stone, the State Trooper that gives driver's license tests, shook my hand."

"Then what?" I whispered.

"Mayor Purdy handed me a gold key to the city, and Mr. Culpepper snapped my picture for the Times-Journal. The mayor hung a gold-framed copy of my picture in the courthouse lobby with a gold plaque underneath saying: Mark Franklin Watson, Fort Payne, Alabama Hero."

REFLECTIONS

A POINT TO PONDER

Mark imagined becoming a hometown hero. What are your big dreams?

A PEARL FROM GOD

"Now to Him who is able to do immeasurably more than all we ask or imagine, according to His power that is at work within us, to Him be glory in the church and in Christ Jesus throughout all generations, for ever and ever! Amen." (Ephesians 3:20-21 NIV)

A PRINCIPLE TO LIVE BY

Commit your imaginations unto the Lord, the One who is able to give you big dreams and make them come true. *"Take delight in the LORD, and He will give you your heart's desires. Commit everything you do to the LORD. Trust Him, and He will help you." (Psalm 37:4-5 NLT)*

Chapter 8:

Friends Forever

"...a real friend sticks closer than a brother."
(Proverbs 18:24 NLT)

The next morning, Mark popped up with the sun and ran to the playroom for Saturday morning cartoons on the black-and-white Zenith Console. Rocky turned toward the wall and kept snoring. "Captain Kangaroo" was over and "Mighty Mouse" had just rescued Pearl Pureheart when I crawled up on the couch beside him, rubbing the sleep from my eyes.

"I'm hungry," I said with a yawn.

Mama set a plate of buttered toast and two steaming bowls of oatmeal mixed with apple sauce, brown sugar, and melted butter on the small table between the couch and the TV. Eating breakfast by the television was a Saturday-morning treat. Our family normally gathered in the kitchen around a wooden picnic table with a lazy Susan in the center. Wooden benches lined three sides of the table pushed against a window with a backyard view. Rocky and Mark shared the left bench. Mama and I shared the front bench. Daddy sat on the right bench. A percolator bubbling a brew of A&P coffee always sat beside his plate. When company came, Mama scooted over next to Daddy, and the company sat by me.

"Mama, what can we do today?" I asked.

"Well, I have a surprise. The Igous have invited us to swim at their house this afternoon."

~

Dr. Igou was our family doctor as well as Daddy's long-time friend. He liked telling the story about Daddy and him at the bottom of a sweaty pile of football players in a high school game. He'd laugh and say, "Watson saw a foot by his head and gave it a twist. You could have heard that knee pop all the way to

Valley Head. And wouldn't you know it, the referee called the penalty on *me*!"

Mrs. Igou had also been a classmate in their Fort Payne High School class of 1939. Dr. Igou bragged that the first time he saw that pretty Carden girl get on the school bus, he told the boy beside him, "I'm gonna marry that girl one day."

He and Daddy went to the University of Alabama after high school and were students there when Pearl Harbor was bombed on December 7, 1941. Dr. Igou went on to medical school at Emory University in Atlanta before serving with the US Army at the Gorgas Hospital in the Panama Canal Zone. Daddy graduated from Alabama and went straight to Officers Candidate School at Camp Davis, Wilmington, North Carolina. He served as an army officer overseas in the Philippines, New Guinea, and Japan. After the war, he returned to Tuscaloosa for law school at the University.

Back in Fort Payne, Dr. Igou's medical office stood on the north end of Gault Avenue, and Daddy's law office sat upstairs over Fort Payne Hardware Store in the heart of town—the best seats around for the annual Christmas parade.

The Igous had three children—Richard, Susan, and Mary. Susan and Rocky had been classmates since Mrs. Hulsey's kindergarten in the basement of Dr. Killian's office building. Halfway through their seventh-grade year at Forest Avenue Elementary School, the entire building shifted a foot over one weekend. So, for the remainder of the year, classes were held at the First Methodist Church. The next fall, Susan and Rocky moved to Williams Avenue School for eighth grade.

Mary Igou was my best friend in the whole wide world. Born just six days apart, we had been friends forever and knew each other's house so well that we could play riddle-ma-riddle-Marie (eye spy) over the *telephone*.

She knew that my favorite Golden Book as a preschooler was *Little Galoshes*. I knew that her favorite of all books was *The Buttercup Fairy* by Cam, and that Mrs. Young at the county library helped her check it out practically every week.

For both families, trips to the library came as regularly as the colored comics in the Sunday edition of the Birmingham News. Every Wednesday afternoon, Mama took us kids to the DeKalb County Library in the basement of the City Hall where Mrs. Annie Young worked the front desk and Mrs. Mary Weatherly ran the show.

Mrs. Weatherly liked telling children the library's history. She said that Fort Payne's first city library had been set up on the second floor of the Opera House back in the Boom Days; but it was not maintained after the mines failed. In 1930, during the Great Depression, Mrs. Weatherly herself had re-established a book room in the upstairs of the Masonic Building. Ten years later, when the 400 volumes had grown to 4,000, the library was moved to the basement of City Hall.

~

That steamy June afternoon at the Igou's house, all the grownups—the Igous, the Cardens (Mrs. Igou's brother and sister-in-law), and Daddy and Mama—sat in the shade of an awning shelling field peas while the kids splashed in the pool. The teenagers flipped from the springboard, Mark swam along the bottom in his oversized googles, and Mary and I played dibble-dabble in the shallow end. Mary's thick, wavy hair wrapped into a tight bun like a ballerina. My short bangs and pageboy stuck to my head like a dark, wet mop. Duchess, the Igou's collie, circled the chain link fence and barked at all the hullabaloo.

Later, Dr. Igou cut two watermelons on the back patio by the swing set, and Mrs. Igou passed out the red, juicy wedges. I leaned over and whispered in Mary's ear, "I know a secret."

REFLECTIONS

A POINT TO PONDER

In this chapter, we learn that Dr. Igou and my daddy were long-time friends. Do you have a long-time friend?

A PEARL FROM GOD

"Two people are better off than one, for they can help each other succeed. If one person falls, the other can reach out and help. But someone who falls alone is in real trouble." (Ecclesiastes 4:9-10 NLT)

A PRINCIPLE TO LIVE BY

Long-time friendships are built and kept by effort and unconditional love. Become a long-time friend by loving, helping, encouraging, and supporting your friends in good times and bad.

Chapter 9:

The Sunday Rule

"Train up a child in the way he should go; even when he is old, he will not depart from it."

(Proverbs 22:6 NASB)

In Sunday School the next morning at the First Methodist Church, I sat beside Mary on the front row of small wooden chairs. (Rocky, Mark, and I didn't fuss about going to church on Sundays—first of all, because we liked it, and second, because of the Watson-Sunday rule: If you didn't feel like *going* to church Sunday morning, then you didn't feel like *playing* Sunday afternoon.)

Daddy had shined my black, patent-leather shoes before we left the neighborhood. With my white-gloved hands, I smoothed the full skirt of last spring's Easter dress—a cantaloupe-colored frock that Mama seamed together on her new Pfaff sewing machine. Two appliquéd butterflies brightened the square sailor collar. Mama and I had picked out the taffeta material and Butterick dress pattern at the Mill End Store on First Street.

Mrs. Shugart plucked the piano keys while Mrs. Crow and Mrs. Cobble led the children singing:

This is my Father's world

And to my listening ears

All nature sings, and round me rings

The music of the spheres.

After a chorus of "Jesus Loves Me" and "Into My Heart," Mrs. Shugart handed Patricia (Freddy and Steve's first cousin) a small plastic church with a slit for coins in the top. She dropped in a dime and passed the offering bank to Mary, who passed it to me, and on it went to each girl and boy in the room.

Following the offering, the teachers divided us into groups by grade, and the soon-to-be second graders followed Mrs. Lackey into a side classroom.

"Children, what do you think it means to be a good neighbor?" Mrs. Lackey asked.

Becky raised her hand.

"Yes, Becky?"

"If your neighbor needs help, you help him," Becky said.

"Good, Becky. Yes, a good neighbor is a helper. Anyone else?"

"You're supposed to love your neighbor like you love yourself," Paul said, "and treat them the way you wanna be treated."

"Very good, Paul. That's exactly right," Mrs. Lackey said. "And a good neighbor puts others before himself."

Mary leaned over and whispered, "When can I see that magic chest of drawers?"

"Maybe this afternoon," I whispered back.

"Girls, no whispering," Mrs. Lackey said. "Let's pay attention to the lesson, please. In the Gospel of Luke, Jesus told a parable. A parable is an earthly story with a heavenly meaning. In His story about a good Samaritan, Jesus hoped to teach His followers how to be a good neighbor. He said, 'Once upon a time, a man was traveling from Jerusalem to Jericho, and he was attacked by robbers...'"

~

After Sunday School, families migrated to their regular seats on curved wooden pews in the beautiful sanctuary. Colorful stained-glass windows hung like jewels on the walls, and deep-maroon carpet covered the floor.

Our family sat on the left side of the center aisle, the Igous sat on the right side, and the Eberharts claimed their spot in the balcony. Our pastor, Travis Warlick, took his place in an oversized wooden chair behind the left pulpit. Mrs. White, the organist, and an impressive pipe organ sat behind him. Until time to stand and sing, the choir director (another Mrs. Watson) and the choir sat behind the right-hand pulpit.

I locked my fingers and silently recited: *Here's the church, here's the steeple, open the door and here's the people. Here's the ladies. Here's the men. One, two, three, four, five, six, seven, eight, nine, ten.* My feet dangled between the pew and the floor and swung back and forth, back and forth. A pat on my leg was Mama's way of saying, "Be still, Jill."

I sat on my hands and studied the gold cross over the altar and the golden chandeliers hanging from the tall ceiling. My eyes wandered to two stained-glass portraits of Jesus on either side of the cross—the Good Shepherd holding a little lamb and the crimson-robed Jesus knocking on a closed wooden door. Jesus's kind eyes seemed to look back into mine. I almost waved.

"All rise," Brother Warlick announced.

The congregation stood and prayed in unison, "Our Father, which art in heaven, hallowed be Thy name. Thy kingdom come, Thy will be done on earth as it is in heaven...."

~

Back in the neighborhood, while Mama prepared lunch, Mary and I skipped outside to pick fresh mint growing under a faucet. Sweet iced tea with spearmint and lemon slices was a Sunday-lunch custom at our house. Every other meal and in-between, our parents made us kids drink milk. Daddy believed that our over-the-top milk consumption was the reason Dr. Brewer never found cavities in our teeth.

Mama set a bowl of creamed potatoes and a hot pan of buttermilk biscuits on the lazy Susan next to the gravy boat and a platter of sliced roast beef and tender carrots. (Every now and then when she cooked white rice instead of potatoes, Daddy would always say, "It sure has been a long time since we've had creamed potatoes.")

We all joined hands, and Daddy prayed, "Dear Lord, bless this food to the nourishment of our bodies and our hands to Thy service. In Christ's name we pray, Amen."

~

After lunch, Mary and I sat on the back patio petting Mama Cat.

"Let's take her back to your room and play dress up," Mary said.

"The parakeets and the fish in the tank are the only animals Mama lets in our house," I said and then grinned. "*But* she never said *you* couldn't bring Mama Cat inside."

Mary hid the cat behind her back. Mama Cat's long tail dragged across the blue tile floor as she side stepped through the kitchen. Mama stood at the sink washing dishes and never turned around.

"Yes, ma'am," we muttered and tossed the cat out the back door. (I think mothers really do have eyes in the back of their heads.)

Mary and I pulled Mama's old skirts, high heels, and sparkly clip-on earbobs from the closet and played dress up in my room. When that game got old, we hid under a blanket, and Mark jumped out of the closet making scary faces over and over again. We screamed every time.

"Wanna go outside?" I asked Mary.

"Sure. Let's go up in the treehouse," she said.

For Mark's sixth birthday, Daddy had built a treehouse atop four tall creosote poles in the backyard. We climbed the ladder, opened the trapdoor, and stepped into the roof-covered, open-air fort or castle tower or whatever we imagined it to be that day. Benches jutted from the walls on either side. Mary and I perched on one side, and Mark sat across from us. From our bird's-eye view, we could see Granddaddy Eberhart's pond to the east, and to the west, Fort Payne stretched down the valley with Sand Mountain as a backdrop.

Mary nudged me. "Ask him," she said.

"Ask me what?" Mark said.

"Can we go see that magic chest of drawers in Grandmother Eberhart's attic?" Mary asked.

"*Secret* chest," I corrected.

Mark glared at me.

Oh boy, I'm in trouble now, I thought.

"Jill! You weren't supposed to tell. You promised."

"But Mary won't tell anybody. Will you, Mary?" I said.

"Cross my heart and hope to die," Mary pledged.

"Freddy's gonna be mad," Mark said.

"He said not to tell *anybody*. Well, Mary's not *anybody*; she's my best friend," I argued. "Come on, let's go see if they're home."

We flip-flopped up the road to house number two in the neighborhood, and found Freddy and Steve riding their bikes on the patio. They traced circles around the oak tree growing in the center.

"She told," Mark announced.

"But, it's okay," I hurriedly explained. "Mary's my best friend, and she won't tell anybody. You won't tell, will you, Mary? And I won't tell anybody else; I promise."

"Chatterbox," Freddy said.

Steve grinned. "Hey, Mary, where's your little lamb?"

"Oh, it followed me to school one day, and I left it there."

Everybody laughed. I felt relieved that Freddy wasn't angry.

"Can I see the magic chest?" Mary asked.

"*Secret* chest," I said again.

"Actually, it's a vintage chest of drawers with a never-solved mystery," Freddy clarified.

"Can I see it?" Mary asked.

"Sure," Freddy said. "Come on."

Freddy, Steve, Mark, Mary, and I marched down the path between house number two and house number one. Halfway in-between, Steve stopped at a big oak on the edge of the brow. "Wanna watch me swing?" he said.

He grabbed a rope that he and Mark had tied around a high limb, backed up for a running go, and then flew over the edge with nothing but air between him and Adamsburg Road down below.

"My turn," I said.

After the boys and I swung from the tree like monkeys on a vine, I offered the rope to Mary. "Wanna try?"

"No, thanks," Mary said. "Y'all are crazy."

REFLECTIONS

A POINT TO PONDER

Was I a good neighbor when I broke my promise and told Freddy's secret?

A PEARL FROM GOD

"A gossip goes around telling secrets, but those who are trustworthy can keep a confidence." (Proverbs 11:13 NLT) "Too much talk leads to sin. Be sensible and keep your mouth shut." (Proverbs 10:19 NLT)

A PRINCIPLE TO LIVE BY

Be a trustworthy friend who keeps your promises.

Chapter 10:

Ting!

"I heard a sound from heaven...like the sound of many harpists." (Revelation 14:2 NLT)

Inside house number one, Grandmother Eberhart and Aunt Evelyn stood by the stove in the smaller kitchen that smelled like a bakery. Grandmother Eberhart smiled. "Hello, children. Would you like a chocolate chip cookie? We just took a batch out of the oven."

"Yes, ma'am!"

"So, what are y'all up to this afternoon?" Aunt Evelyn said.

"Mary-had-a-little-lamb wants to see the chest of drawers," Steve said.

Grandmother Eberhart's eyes twinkled. "Oh, you do," she said.

"Yes, ma'am," Mary answered. "Jill said it's magic."

"I said it's a *secret*," I said.

"Mrs. Eberhart," Mark asked, "how did it get in your attic?"

"You children come sit at the table to eat your cookies, and I'll tell you the whole story," Grandmother Eberhart said sweetly.

I mumbled through a mouth full of cookie, "Freddy already told us a really *long* story about the coal mines and a rich lady and a big fire."

"What happened after the fire?" Mark asked.

"I was just a girl at the time, not quite nine years old, but I remember the night of the fire just like it was yesterday," she said. "The blazes shot up so high that the whole sky over Fort Payne looked like day was dawning. My daddy was a volunteer fireman and hurried over to try to help save it, but that big hotel went up in flames like a box of matches."

"How come the chest of drawers didn't burn up?" Steve asked.

"Oh, honey, it would have burned slap up if it hadn't been for two brave men that slid it onto a blanket and pulled it out the front door. When they it got outside, Daddy and others joined together and carried the heavy chest down the front steps. The men tried to go back inside for more things, but by then, the lobby was an inferno."

"What's an inferno?" I asked.

"A fire that's out of control," Freddy explained.

"What started it?" Mark asked.

"They think a candle fell against the curtains in one of the rooms. One tiny flame started a giant firestorm. Folks lined Gault Avenue all night long and watched the DeKalb Hotel burn to the ground. At daybreak the next morning, the men loaded the chest onto Daddy's truck—a black Ford Model TT, one of the first pickups ever made in America. The mayor asked him to keep it at our house until he could figure out what to do with it."

"Did you look for the unseen beauty?" Mark asked.

"I sure did. Combed every stitch of that chest of drawers from top to bottom, but never found a thing. Well, time marched on as time does. I grew up and got married and had young'uns of my own. After Daddy and Mama died, we cleaned out the old house and found that chest still sittin' in the basement. We liked to have never gotten that heavy thing into the attic. Freddy and Steve's granddaddy and Jimmy and Norman had to use a cable and pulley to get it up there."

~

The attic felt as hot as blue blazes. Mark and Steve poked through a basket of rusty tools. Freddy sat in the tattered rocker and strummed an old guitar with a broken string. I pulled Mary by the hand. "Over here," I said.

Mary looked around. "It's kinda spooky up here, and really hot, too."

I pointed to the chest. "Well, there it is. Came all the way across the ocean from Germany."

Mary touched a tarnished-green knight. Steve snuck up behind her and hollered, "Boo!"

We both jumped and squealed. Mary's shoulder bumped the chest.

TING.

"What was that?" I said.

"What was what?" Mark asked.

"That tinkling sound. Like a harp or something," I said.

"I didn't hear anything. You probably just heard Freddy playin' that old guitar," Mark said.

"I heard it, too," Mary said.

"Silly girls," Steve chimed.

"Maybe you heard an *angel*," Freddy whispered.

My eyes shot toward the ceiling. The boys laughed. They thought it was funny. I didn't.

REFLECTIONS

A POINT TO PONDER

What started the fire at the DeKalb Hotel? Did you know that God compares our words to a roaring fire?

A PEARL FROM GOD

"Indeed, we all make many mistakes. For if we could control our tongues, we would be perfect and could control ourselves in every other way...the tongue is a small thing that makes grand speeches. But a tiny spark can set a great forest on fire. And among all the parts of the body the tongue is a flame of fire. It is a whole world of wickedness, corrupting your entire body. It can set your whole life on fire...blessing and cursing come pouring out of the same mouth. Surely, my brothers and sisters, this is not right!" (James 3:2-10 NLT)

A PRINCIPLE TO LIVE BY

Words can bless or destroy. Therefore, be careful little tongue what you say, for the Father up above is looking down with love. Use your words to encourage one another and build each other up.

Chapter 11:

Fourth of July

"For you have been called to live in freedom, my brothers and sisters."   (Galatians 5:13 NLT)

At the crack of dawn four days later, I skipped down the hall to Mark and Rocky's room. "Wake up, sleepy heads!" I shouted. "It's the Fourth of July!"

Routinely, local businesses around Fort Payne closed Thursday and Saturday afternoons and all-day Sundays, but, today, the whole town would shut down to celebrate Independence Day (with the exceptions of the Hamilton Drive-in, home of Fort Payne's slam-bang fireworks show, and the firemen who supervised the annual event).

"It's gonna be a great day!" I cried.

"Go away," Rocky muttered and crammed his pillow over his head.

"Daddy's grilling hamburgers and we're making homemade peppermint ice cream and Uncle Frank and Aunt Jo and baby Vicki are coming over and we're gonna see fireworks tonight at the drive-in."

~

Uncle Frank, Aunt Jo, and baby Vicki lived on the broad top of Lookout Mountain just a few miles from our neighborhood at the Nance-family farm on Fruit Farm Road. They raised cattle, grew a big summer garden, and kept three ponds stocked full of bass, bream, and catfish.

Uncle Frank and Daddy were half-brothers. When Daddy was only three years old and his baby sister, Dot, was on the way, their father died of the flu in Akron, Ohio. After his death, Grandmama and Daddy rode a train back to Alabama. Six years later, she married Floyd Nance, and when Daddy was twelve, Frank was born.

~

On the back patio, Rocky, Mark, and I took turns cranking the ice cream churn while we listened to Daddy and Uncle Frank tell stories. Daddy flipped the Nance-farm ground-beef patties on the stone barbeque pit and said, "One time, when I was about ten, all my friends were going camping, and Dad asked why I wasn't going. When I told him that I didn't have any camping equipment, he took me to the store straight away and bought a tent and a sleeping bag. That was a big deal to me as a kid, but it means even more now that I understand that Alabama was in the throes of the Great Depression at the time."

"Yeah," Frank said, "I only remember bits and pieces from those hard years. Grandmaw Robison told me they were flat broke. She needed a pair of new shoes and tried to borrow a dime from her brother, but he wouldn't give it to her. She vowed then and there that if they ever got out of that deep hole of poverty, she'd never let 'em hit the bottom of the barrel again. I reckon half of everything Grandpaw made after that went into Grandmaw's cookie jar for a rainy day."

"Speaking of rainy days," Daddy said, "do you think it's gonna rain out the fireworks tonight? I see a thunderhead building over Sand Mountain."

I silently prayed, *Lord, pleeease, don't let it rain out the fireworks tonight.*

"Maybe not," Uncle Frank said. "You know they say the biggest fireworks show Fort Payne ever saw was back in the Boom Days."

"Well, they say the biggest *fire* Fort Payne ever saw was back when the DeKalb Hotel burned to the ground," I chirped.

Both men stared at me like I had four eyes. "How'd you know about that, sugar?" Daddy asked.

"Grandmother Eberhart told us the *whole* story," I blabbered. "Her daddy was a fireman and helped save the secret ch…"

Mark started tickling me to hush me up just as Mama came out the door carrying baked beans and a large bowl of homemade potato salad. I squealed, "STOP it, Mark!"

"Mark, leave your sister alone," she said.

When she turned her back, I stuck my tongue out at him.

Aunt Jo followed Mama. She held baby Vicki on her hip and two bags of Colonial hamburger buns in her hand. They set the food on the rock picnic table beside a platter stacked with grilled burgers. Mama pulled cold 6 oz. coca colas from the ice chest and said, "Time to eat. Winfred, will you say the blessing, please?"

~

That evening, Mark and I waited on the piano bench in the living room while Mama and Daddy got ready to go to the drive-in. Rocky had ridden his bike down the mountain to Jeff's house, a friend who lived on Forest Avenue half a block from Grandmama and Granddaddy.

"Jill, I love you no matter what," Mark lectured, "but other kids aren't gonna want to play with you or be your friend if you keep acting mean and breaking promises."

I glared at the black and white keys on the apartment grand piano. My lips pouted. "I'm not mean," I muttered.

"Most of the time you're sweet. But you argue about everything, and when you make a promise, you need to keep it."

My insides felt all wrong—a jumble of sad and mad, embarrassed and defensive, but I knew he was right. Breaking promises didn't make me a kind neighbor like the good Samaritan, and I really wasn't treating my friends the way I wanted to be treated. Self-defense slowly melted into repentance.

"I'm sorry, Mark. I'll try to do better," I said.

He hugged me.

"Okay, kids, let's go!" Daddy called.

~

The drive-in sat on the corner of Drinkard Drive and Gault Avenue at the north end of town. The Hamilton family had opened the outdoor 400-car-capacity theater in May, 1950. The first movie played that spring was "It's a Great Feeling," starring Doris Day.

Daddy pulled beside the ticket booth and paid the cashier $2.50 for the four of us.

"Would you like a box of popcorn, sir," the young lady asked.

"No, thank you," Daddy replied, knowing a paper bag full sat on the floorboard beside Mama's feet. She claimed that home-popped corn tasted much better, but truth be told, homemade snacks saved money.

He pulled the 1957 Ford Custom 300 to the middle of row E and hung a speaker on the window. The Walt Disney Productions family musical "Summer Magic" starring Hayley Mills and Burl Ives was just starting.

Mark and I giggled as Mr. Ives crooned:

"Once a lonely caterpillar sat and cried,

To a sympathetic beetle by his side.

"I've got nobody to hug,

I'm such an ugly bug.

Then a spider and dragon fly replied,

"If you're serious and want to win a bride,

Come along with us,

To the glorious

Annual ugly bug ball.

"Come on let's crawl

Gotta crawl, gotta crawl

To the ugly bug ball

To the ball, to the ball

And a happy time we'll have there

One and all

At the ugly bug ball."

After the movie, we perched on the sage-green hood for a clear view. Ignited missiles shot into the night sky and exploded into glittering umbrellas of color.

BANG!

BOOM!

BANG ricocheted down the valley, bouncing between Lookout Mountain and Sand Mountain. Smoke and the stinky smell of burnt sulfur choked the air. The show ended with red, white, and blue sparkles in the shape of the American flag and the Niagara-Falls grand finale—a long shower of white firelights stretched across the drive-in pond. Claps and whistles and cheers followed the dazzling concert.

I clapped and yelled, "Bravo! Bravo!"

Daddy, Mama, and Mark laughed at me, but I didn't mind.

REFLECTIONS

A POINT TO PONDER

When Grandmaw Robison needed help buying shoes, did her brother help her?

A PEARL FROM GOD

"If someone has enough money to live well and sees a brother or sister in need but shows no compassion—how can God's love be in that person? Dear children, let's not merely say that we love each other; let us show the truth by our actions." (1 John 3:17-18 NLT)

A PRINCIPLE TO LIVE BY

God blesses us so that we may be a blessing to others. Be ready and willing and happy to share what you have with people in need. Be a helper.

Chapter 12:

Who Knows?

"I pray that you will keep on growing in knowledge and understanding." (Philippians 1:9 NLT)

On Friday, Mark and I went to Granddaddy and Grandmama's house to spend the night. When it grew too dark to play outside, we ran inside the house and raced to the basement. He dashed into the linen closet in the bathroom and slid down the laundry shoot. I ran to a door in the hallway and flew down the wooden stairs. (I was too chicken to take the laundry shaft.) Mark was standing by a 1940 Maytag wringer washing machine when I bounded from the last step.

"Beat you!" he said.

I started to stick out my tongue but remembered the "do unto others" talk and said instead, "You were fast! Wanna skate?"

We strapped roller skates onto our Keds and wheeled around the cellar to the concrete culvert—a section of the town's underground drainage system that ran along the back wall. (In a downpour one spring, the concrete lid had lifted off the conduit, flooding the basement. Grandmama had run outdoors and smashed the basement windows with a hammer to keep the water from rising into the main floor. Needless to say, Fort Payne's Water and Sanitation Department helped pay for the damages.)

"Y'all want a snack?" Grandmama called down the stairwell.

"Yes, ma'am!"

In the living room, the pungent odor of pipe tobacco drifted from Granddaddy's brown leather chair. Mark and I sprawled on the floor in front of the television, dipping bananas into a small bowl of Blue Ribbon mayonnaise and watching Granddaddy's favorite Western, "Rawhide," starring Eric Fleming as

Gil Favor and Clint Eastwood as Rowdy Yates. When the program ended, it was bath time.

Because homes in town had the luxury of city water, Grandmama drew a deep bath and scrubbed me from head to toe with Ivory soap. When I was spick and span, dried and dressed in baby-doll pajamas, Mark ran a second tub full and scrubbed himself as clean as a whistle.

Grandmama read to us before we fell asleep. Mark and I sat in the middle of the double bed in the bedroom behind the kitchen and listened to "Little Orphant Annie" by James Whitcomb Riley—our favorite poem in Miriam Blanton Huber's <u>Story and Verse for Children</u>:

"Little Orphant Annie's come to our house to stay,

An' wash the cups an' saucers up,

an' brush the crumbs away,

An' shoo the chickens off the porch,

an' dust the hearth an' sweep,

An' make the fire, an' bake the bread,

an' earn her board-an'-keep;

An' all us other children,

when the supper-things is done,

We set around the kitchen fire an'

has the mostest fun…"

She turned the page with gnarled fingers, twisted out of shape by softball games not old age. (Grandmama taught third and fourth graders at the same time in the same classroom at Fischer Elementary School on Lookout Mountain. At recess, she insisted on pitching for both teams and had broken a finger more than once catching hard-hit balls without a mitt.)

At the end of the poem, she said, "Time to say our prayers." We folded our hands and prayed together:

"Now I lay me down to sleep,

I pray the Lord my soul to keep;

If I should die before I wake,

I pray the Lord my soul to take.

Amen."

Grandmama planted kisses on our cheeks. "Sleep tight and don't let the bed bugs bite," she said.

"Grandmama?" Mark said.

"Yes, sugar?"

"Do you remember when the DeKalb Hotel burned down?" Mark asked.

"I sure do," she said. "I was a teenager at the time."

"Did you see it burn?" he asked.

"No, I didn't see the fire that night because my family didn't live in Fort Payne back then. But a few days after the fire, Papa brought us up here. I remember the hotel was nothing but a big pile of smoldering rubble. Why do you ask?"

"Freddy and Steve's Grandmother Eberhart told us about it, and I was just wondering," he said. "Good night."

"Night-night, sugar," she said and turned off the light.

Crickets sang through the open window. A street light in the alley glowed through the lace curtains.

"Mark," I whispered. "Did you break the promise?"

"No," he said. "We promised not to tell anybody about the chest of drawers. Most old folks in town already know about the fire."

"Oh, okay, good," I said. "Night-night."

"Good night, Jill."

~

The next morning, we lay on our bellies in front of the television again. Dust specks danced in the sunbeams streaming through the windows. Pots and pans rattled in the kitchen where Grandmama and Aunt Dot were cooking breakfast. Roy Rogers and Dale Evans plotted across the black and white screen on horseback singing:

"Happy trails to you,

Until we meet again.

Happy trails to you,

Keep smiling until then…"

"It's ready," Grandmama called from the breakfast room.

The cheerful breakfast room sat between the kitchen and the dining room. Bright sunshine poured through a large window onto the white table covered with a yellow cloth. After the blessing, Mark and I dug into crispy bacon, scrambled eggs, buttery grits, and buttermilk biscuits heaped on floral china plates.

"How'd you kids sleep last night?" Grandmama said.

"Good," Mark said.

"Sugar, did Mrs. Eberhart happen to mention a fancy chest of drawers when she told you about the fire at the DeKalb Hotel?" Grandmama Nance said.

Mark's jaw dropped. I looked bug-eyed.

"You *know* about the secret chest of drawers?" Mark said.

REFLECTIONS

A POINT TO PONDER

Why did I *not* stick out my tongue at Mark when he won the race to the basement?

A PEARL FROM GOD

"My children, listen when your father corrects you. Pay attention and learn good judgment, for I am giving you good guidance. Don't turn away from my instructions… Get wisdom; develop good judgment. Don't forget my words or turn away from them." (Proverbs 4:1-2,5 NLT)

A PRINCIPLE TO LIVE BY

Follow wise advice and learn from your mistakes. God says if you do this—store wisdom in your heart and live by it—you will live many years, and your life will be satisfying.

Chapter 13:

Grandmaw's Story

"You will be able to tell wonderful stories to your children and grandchildren about the marvelous things I am doing." (Exodus 10:2 NLT)

I sat between Grandmama and Mark on the front seat of the 1961 Mercury Monterey headed down the valley toward Collinsville at a snail's pace.

"Grandmama, *please* tell us how you know about the old chest?" Mark begged again.

She smiled. "It's Mama's story. I'll let her tell it when we get there."

"Grandmama, why do drive so slow?" I asked.

"Do you remember what happened to me last year in my old, black car?" she said.

"Your brakes gave out going down the mountain," Mark said.

"Mr. Abbott said it sounded like a freight train flyin' by his house," I said. "How'd you stop?"

"I cried, 'Help me, Lord Jesus!' and then turned the wheel toward the bank, but I was going so fast the car just bounced off the kudzu and right back on the road," she said. "Thank the good Lord, it stopped when I hit the bank a second time. It 'bout scared me to my grave. That's why I drive so slowly nowadays."

"I'm glad you didn't get hurt," Mark said.

Farms lined the highway between Fort Payne and Collinsville. Mark and I searched for horses in every pasture. Rocky spent all his wishes on water, but not Mark and me. Every birthday, Christmas, and evening star, we wished for a horse.

"There's one, and it has a baby," Mark said, pointing to a chestnut mare and a spindly-legged colt.

"I wish we had a horse," I said. "Grandmama, are we there yet?"

"Just a few more minutes, sugar," she said.

Minutes that seemed like hours later, we rolled into Collinsville, turned left off Highway 11 onto McClain Street, then made an immediate right onto College Avenue. Halfway down the block, we turned left into the driveway of Grandpaw and Grandmaw Robison's brown cobblestone house.

Grandmama found Grandmaw busy in the kitchen. She kissed her and walked back to the bedroom to speak to Grandpaw, now bedridden and, according to Daddy, as nutty as a fruit cake.

Mark and I watched Grandmaw pour heavy cream into a yellow mixture of sugar and eggs. "Whatcha makin'?" I asked.

"Freezer cream," Grandmaw said. She added a pinch of salt and a teaspoon of vanilla flavoring, stirred it with a wooden spoon, and set the metal bowl inside the freezer.

"Now, we'll have some ice cream to go with our pound cake." She opened a cabinet and pulled out a cigar box filled with wooden pegs, thread spools, and darning eggs. "You children want to play with these little pigs?" she said.

"Why do you call 'em pigs?" I asked.

Her almond-shaped eyes crinkled, and her mouth curved to a wide smile, accenting high-cheek bones, a characteristic of her Native-American ancestors. (Grandmaw's grandmother, Unity Brown Beason, was born in 1834 and, because she was half Cherokee, her grandkids called her "Indian Grandmother." Unity's parents were David Brown and Susan Battles Brown. We reckon that Susan must have been the full-blooded Native American. Grandmaw would say with a twinkle in her eye, "My great-grandparents married two diverse nations and created *Unity*.")

She picked up a wooden darning egg painted pink. "Doesn't this look like a little piggy to you?"

I grinned. "Yes, ma'am."

"Grandmama said you know a story about that fancy chest of drawers that used to be in the DeKalb Hotel," Mark said.

"Will you tell us the story?" I begged. "P*leeease,* Grandmaw?"

"My, my that was so long ago. Let me think. Well, I was born in St. Clair County near Whitney to Miller and

Betty Beason, your great-great grandparents," she said. "I was just about your age, Mark, when Fort Payne's Boom Days began. Those were magical times for us country kids that had hardly seen the outside of a barn. Folks came pouring into town like rainwater down a drainpipe."

"Freddy told us all about that," I said.

Mark put his finger to his lips.

I quickly added, "But you can tell us again."

Grandmaw patted my hand. "Well, Papa farmed in the spring, summer, and fall, but in the wintertime, he cut and sold firewood to put food on the table, and the new rich folks in Fort Payne were his *best* customers. They paid an extra 15¢ if Papa stacked a pile of wood inside by the fireplace. I liked going with him on his deliveries when it wasn't too wet or cold."

"In February of 18...let me think, 1891, I believe it was, Papa and I made a trip to Fort Payne. The Boom Days were winding down by then and lots of folks had just packed up and left. We stopped at Mrs. Higgins's home on Grand Avenue to deliver a load of hand-split logs. She was a grand, old lady that lived in a large, grand house."

I giggled. "A *grand* lady in a *grand* house on *Grand* Avenue?"

Grandmaw Robison chuckled. Like our daddy, her shoulders shook up and down when she laughed. "Now, wasn't that *grand*!" she said. "Mrs. Higgins was a musician from Boston, and she had a *grand* piano in her parlor."

I cackled. "Did she have any *grand*kids?"

"Well, no, she didn't. As a matter of fact, she was a widow with no children at all. Anyway, Mrs. Higgins asked Papa if I could stay and help her with some household chores while he made the rest of his deliveries that day. She promised to pay me a whole dollar if I did. So, Papa consented and said he'd be back in a couple of hours to fetch me."

"I worked hard. Scrubbed floors. Swept the hearth. Shook out rugs. Dusted the parlor and living room and dining room. Washed dishes. And when I figured I was just about done, Mrs. Higgins said she had saved a special job for last. She handed me a stack of rags and a bowl of paste made of vinegar and flour and salt and just a dab of oil, and then she led me to a large bedroom with a four-poster bed. A fringed, rose-colored canopy covered the top. I thought it was the most elegant thing I had ever laid eyes on until I turned around. Then, I saw it: a magnificent, carved-walnut chest of drawers. Oh, my, it was fine. Mrs. Higgins opened a drawer and let me feel the…"

"Royal-blue felt!" I cried.

"Why, yes, sugar, that's right! And on the top, there were three bronze knights on horseback dressed in shining armor. Mrs. Higgins showed me how to carefully apply the vinegar paste to the bronze figurines and polish them shiny-clean with the soft clothes. She told me the chest of drawers was extremely valuable and had belonged to someone of great importance in Stuttgart, Germany—a relative who appreciated the beauty of music even more than she did. About that time, Papa knocked on the door, and we went home. The next time we stopped by, the house was empty. Mrs. Higgins and that enchanting chest of drawers were gone. A neighbor told us she'd moved back to Boston."

"Years passed. I grew up, but I never forgot that beautiful, old chest and the afternoon I spent with Mrs. Higgins. Spring of 1900, I married your grandpaw at the Methodist Church in Odenville. We set up housekeeping in Collinsville and rode up to Fort Payne from time to time to get supplies at the dry-goods store. While we were there one morning, I asked your grandpaw if we could stop by the DeKalb Hotel and take a peek inside. I'd never set foot in that fancy inn before, but I'd always wanted to. So, he parked the wagon under a shade tree in Union Park and hitched the mule to a post. We waltzed across the street and right into the DeKalb Hotel just like we belonged there. And lo and behold, what do you think we spotted sittin' under a crystal chandelier as pretty as you please?"

"The chest of drawers!" Mark and I shouted.

"Right as rain. I reckon it sat there till the big fire burned it to ashes with everything else."

"No, ma'am," I told her excitedly, "it didn't burn! It's sittin' in Grandmother Eberhart's attic. We saw it with our own eyes."

Grandmaw threw her hands up in the air. "Well, bless my stars and garters!" she cried. "I can't believe it!"

REFLECTIONS

A POINT TO PONDER

Do you think Grandmaw Robison's story may shed light on the chest of drawers' mystery? Do you know that God says His word (the Bible) sheds light on the mysteries of life?

A PEARL FROM GOD

"Your word is a lamp to guide my feet and a light to my path." (Psalm 119:105 NLT) "My child, listen to what I say and treasure My commands...you will understand what is right, just, and fair, and you will find the right way to go." (Proverbs 2:1,9 NLT)

A PRINCIPLE TO LIVE BY

Read the Bible every day. Look to God and His word for guidance and help through every season of life.

Chapter 14:

Chasing the Wind

"But I learned firsthand that pursuing all this is like chasing the wind." (Ecclesiastes 1:17 NLT)

Daddy was waiting on the screened porch when we got back to Grandmama's house. "We better hurry," he said. "The Bob Brandy Show starts in thirty minutes."

~

Bob Brandy was Chattanooga, Tennessee's own singing cowboy and the host of an after-school kids' television show, which broadcasted from Signal Mountain. Kids in the audience who won a game or sat on Bob's horse, Rebel, got a Moon Pie or a Little Debbie snack as a prize. On Saturdays, Bob took the show on the road with his pretty wife Ingrid and Rebel, of course. Today, Bob Brandy was visiting Fort Payne at the DeKalb Theater.

~

Freddy and Steve had saved Mark and me seats on the fourth row from the front. I sat down beside Freddy, and Mark sat next to me.

"Thanks for saving us seats," I whispered.

"You're welcome," Freddy said.

Cowboy Bob opened the show with a song and then picked kids from the audience to come on stage for a round of "Popeye Says." I couldn't believe it when he chose me!

On stage, Cowboy Bob shouted, "Popeye says, 'Put your hands on your head.'"

I put my hands on my hips and so did the little boy beside me. Cowboy Bob laughed. "You two need to learn where your head is. I'm sorry; you're out. Go sit down, now."

I defended my case. "But I thought you said *hips*."

The boy nodded. "Me, too."

"What do you think, boys and girls? Should we give them a second chance?" Cowboy Bob asked.

"YES!!!" the audience screamed.

Cowboy Bob let us stay, and I wound up winning the game and the prize: a carton of 6 oz. bottled coca-colas.

"Before you get your prize," he said, "you have to kiss Cowboy Bob on the cheek."

(For years, I bragged about kissing Bob Brandy once upon a time.)

~

Back in the neighborhood, Mark hung a canteen around his neck. "Her name was Mrs. Higgins, and she was a musician," he told Freddy and Steve. "Here, Jill, you carry the buns and marshmallows and stuff."

I grabbed the paper sack. "And we didn't tell," I said. "Promise! Grandmama just asked us out of the blue if your grandmother knew about the chest of drawers."

"Well, not exactly out of the blue," Mark said. "I asked her if she remembered the hotel fire. That's why she asked us about the chest of drawers."

Steve carried four wire coat-hangers in one hand and a heavy canvas knapsack swollen with kindling on his back. "Did you get the matches?" he asked.

"Got 'em," Freddy said and held up a bag. "In here with the hot dogs, mustard, and ketchup. What else did she say?"

"Mrs. Higgins was a *grand* lady that lived in a *grand* house on *Grand* Avenue, and she had a *grand* piano but no kids or *grand*kids," I said.

"You're kidding," Freddy said.

"Nope, I'm serious. That's what Grandmaw said. Didn't she, Mark?"

"Yep, and she told Grandmaw that the chest was worth a lot of money, and it once belonged to somebody *really* important in Stuttgart, Germany," Mark said.

"Somebody kin to her," I added, "that liked music."

"Yeah, she said that whoever it was appreciated the beauty of music more than she did," Mark said.

"The *beauty of music*. That could be a clue," Steve said.

We traipsed down the chert road between house number four and house number five in the neighborhood, crossed the creek, and climbed a steep hill to a path cutting through the woods to Big Rock—our name for the rocky bluff overlooking Fort Payne in the valley.

"Did y'all know Fort Payne used to be a Cherokee village called Willstown?" Mark said.

"Then why's it called Fort Payne now?" I asked.

Freddy pointed to the valley. "'Cause the U.S. Army built a fort down there to hold Native Americans being forced to move to Oklahoma, and Major John

Payne was the commanding officer. So, they renamed the town Fort Payne."

"Yeah, and the Cherokees were really sad about movin'. That's why it's called the Trail of Tears," Steve said. "We studied all about it in Alabama history last year. My teacher said that when Fort Payne became a railroad stop between Birmingham and Chattanooga, it started growing fast."

"Oh, okay," I said. "Y'all sure do know a lot of stuff."

Freddy and Steve worked their way down a narrow crack between rock columns.

"Jill, you stay behind me," Mark said, "and go slow."

He led the way. I clung to his shirttail as we scooted down the crevice onto a narrow ledge under the overhang. Freddy and Steve were building a ring of rocks on the bare dirt.

Mark held his hand out at arm's length toward the dropping sun. "We've got about an hour and half till sundown," he announced.

"How'd you know that?" I asked.

"'Cause I closed one eye and counted the number of fingers between the sun and the top of Sand Mountain. Each finger measures about fifteen minutes in sun time, and I counted six-fingers."

"You don't have six fingers," I argued.

"I do if I use both hands. Anyhow, six times fifteen is ninety minutes or an hour and a half," he patiently explained.

"You're smart, Mark," I said.

He pulled a tinder bundle of dried grass, shredded bark, and brown pine straw from a pocket in his blue jeans and set it in the center of the rock circle. Steve placed twigs over the tinder and then built a teepee of kindling above the twigs, leaving a thin opening for airflow. Freddy crouched down, struck a match, and lit the tinder. On hands and knees, we all blew gently until the smoldering bundle ignited the twigs. Fifteen minutes later, the kindling blazed to a campfire ready for cooking.

The boys untwisted the wire hangers into roasting sticks. Mark used his pocket knife to open the package of Oscar Mayer hot dogs and slid a wiener onto a wire for me.

"Don't get it too close to the fire," he said, "or it'll burn."

"Okay," I said.

"And don't touch the end of the wire 'cause it's hot, and it'll burn you," he said.

"Okay."

After eating a ton of hot dogs, we roasted marshmallows over the coals and smashed the golden-brown puffs between graham crackers and Hershey chocolate bars.

I giggled. "Can I have s'more?"

"Silly dill pickle," Steve said.

"Let's go back in the attic tomorrow and search the chest of drawers again," Mark said. "Maybe the *beauty of music* is a clue."

"Yeah, maybe, but we've looked a hundred times already and haven't found anything. It's like trying to find a needle in a haystack," Freddy moaned. "Like chasing the wind."

"Don't give up, Freddy," I said. "You'll figure it, and we'll help you."

"We gotta have faith," Mark said. "Grandmama says that faith is believin' today your hopes and prayers for tomorrow. She says just 'cause something is *unseen* doesn't make it *unreal*."

"You're right. Thanks," Freddy said.

"Okay, y'all, it's time to put out the fire," Mark said.

We emptied the canteens onto the embers and then covered the charred wood with dust.

"Freddy, will you tell us a story?" I begged. "Pleeease!"

Mark looked at the western sky. "We better pack up and head back," he said. "We gotta be home by dark."

The red sun sat on top of Sand Mountain and painted a gold frame around the pink and purple clouds. Lights twinkled through windows in the valley below, and the zing-zing-zing of July flies whirred in the trees above.

"We've got time for a short one," Freddy said. "It'll be a while before it's really dark."

I clapped my hands.

"Once upon a time there was a really, really rich man that lived all alone in a huge mansion on a tiny island in the Pacific Ocean," Freddy began. "He was so rich that his desk was made of solid gold..."

REFLECTIONS

A POINT TO PONDER

How do you think the Native Americans felt when they had to leave their homeland?

A PEARL FROM GOD

"Do not be afraid, for I have ransomed you. I have called you by name; you are mine. When you go through deep waters, I will be with you. When you walk through the fire of oppression, you will not be burned up; the flames will not consume you. For I am the LORD, your God." *(Isaiah 43:1-3 NLT)*

A PRINCIPLE TO LIVE BY

God doesn't promise His kids a pain-free life; He promises to walk with us through the pain. When you feel sad or scared or disappointed, depend on God, the One who loves you and longs to help you.

Chapter 15:

Shelter Number Two

"It will be a shelter from daytime heat and a hiding place from storms and rain."

(Isaiah 4:6 NLT)

The next morning, Mark grabbed one handle of the wooden picnic basket; I grabbed the other. We toted it out to Daddy, and he set the hamper in the back of the jeep beside four folded lawn chairs and a fat water jug.

"But, Daddy, we were going to Grandmother Eberhart's house with Freddy and Steve this morning to search the chest of drawers again," Mark said.

"You can do that another time, sugar," Daddy said. "Today, we're going to DeSoto State Park to celebrate Rocky's fourteenth birthday."

"Yeah, Mark," I twittered, "this'll be way more fun. I *love* the park."

Daddy, Mama, Rocky, his friend, Jeff, Mark, and I packed into the jeep and headed out of the neighborhood. Daddy turned right on Adamsburg Road and drove up the steep hill toward "Five Points."

~

John Eberhart's Grocery sat on the right side of a five-road intersection that everybody called "Five Points." His wife (Granny Eberhart) and their daughter, Patsy, (kinfolks of the Eberharts in house number one and house number two in the neighborhood) ran the store. Two of their grandkids, Frank and Mary Ann, lived just a hop, skip, and a jump away from the store on Dogtown Road. Sometimes, Frank and Mary Ann cut down through the woods to our neighborhood and played with Freddy, Steve, Mark, and me.

Last January, when a winter storm buried the mountain under a blanket of ice and snow, we pulled our sleds to John Eberhart's house on Scenic Road and raced down the hill, across Five Points, and onto Adamsburg Road. We slid to a stop at Frank and Mary Ann's Aunt Gail's house—about a half-mile run and the best sledding ever!

~

Daddy turned left at Five Points onto Scenic Road, drove along the upper brow to Highway 35, then crossed over to DeSoto Parkway.

Up hills.

Down hills.

Past the Culpepper farm.

Past Fischer Elementary School where Grandmama Nance would teach third and fourth graders again in the fall.

Past the calf pens at Scooter Howell's dairy farm with the highest producing jersey herd in America.

"Daddy, why do they put the little calves in pens out by the road?" I asked.

"To get 'em used to traffic," Rocky said.

Jeff laughed.

Rocky grinned. "She'll believe anything," he said under his breath.

Finally, we spotted the DeSoto State Park sign on the right side of the road and the park manager's cabin on the left. The road dropped downhill and curved around a big boulder. At the bottom of the hill, Daddy turned right and climbed another hill to the parking lot for shelter number one where Granddaddy, Grandmama, and Aunt Dot waited at the picnic tables.

Mark and I dashed to the playground. He climbed the ladder of the high slide, and I ran past the see-saws to the tall swings hanging from a crossbeam twenty-feet up in the air.

"Come here, kids," Daddy called. "I want you to meet somebody."

Daddy introduced us to a man beside him wearing hiking boots and khaki pants. "This is Mr. J. O.

Evans, the park manager. J.O., these are two of my kids, Mark and Jill."

"Nice to meet you," Mark said.

"How long have you worked here?" I asked.

"Well, believe it or not, the first time I worked in the park was back in the 1930s with the CCC boys," Mr. Evans said.

"What are the CCC boys?" I asked.

"The Civilian Conservation Corps. During the Depression, President Roosevelt organized the program to give jobs to young men needing work, and, believe me, I sorely needed a job. We planted billions of trees and built trails and walls and bridges and shelters in parks all over the United States. I was assigned to these 3,500-acres of woods, rivers, and waterfalls, and in 1939, DeSoto State Park was dedicated as the largest state park in Alabama," Mr. Evans said proudly. "Do you kids know who the park was named after?"

"A Spanish explorer," Mark said. "Hernando de Soto."

Daddy looked pleased.

"That's right, Mark," Mr. Evans said. "So, today, when you hike the park trails and visit DeSoto Falls, look for the rock structures that I helped build."

"Yes, sir," we said.

"Speaking of hiking, if we're gonna finish a trail before lunch, we better get goin'," Daddy said. "Thanks, J.O., you have a good day."

"You, too, Winfred. Nice to meet you, Mark and Jill."

Our favorite trail started at a huge rock behind the picnic shelter, where Mark and I usually sat to eat peanut-butter-and-jelly sandwiches and Lay's potato chips. From the "picnic" rock, the path cut downhill through the woods toward Little River.

Mark and I raced to a stone drinking fountain for a quick sip of spring water and then trotted down the trail ahead of the rest of the family. Daddy held Grandmama's arm and helped her maneuver the rocky descent to the bluff overlooking the river. We heard the rushing water before we saw it.

"This way," Daddy said, pointing left toward the north fork of the trail.

Sunlight sliced through the thick mountain laurel and rhododendron bushes edging the pathway. On Mother's Day, pink blossoms had dangled from the branches like ornaments on a Christmas tree. Today, the bushes formed a green tunnel. Mark and I plucked tiny, dark-blue berries from a huckleberry bush and popped them in our mouths.

"How do they taste?" Rocky asked.

"A little dry," Mark said. "Kinda like blueberry raisins."

The north trail led to a span of stone steps. "Mama, did you know that Mr. Evans and the CCC boys built these?" I said.

Patches of Little Brown Jugs—wild ginger plants with light-green leaves and dark-green veins—grew alongside. Daddy lifted a heart-shaped leaf and showed us the unusual brown flowers that looked like little jugs.

At the bottom of the steps, the trail veered right onto a wooden bridge over a noisy creek. Emerald moss carpeted the shady banks. Crystal-clear water hopped over rocks and splashed its way into Little River. We crossed the bridge single file.

"Everybody turn around and say cheese," Daddy said.

"Cheese!"

He snapped a picture with the twin-lens Yashica camera strapped around his neck. As we climbed the last hill before shelter number two, the sun disappeared behind a dark cloud, and thunder rumbled in the distance.

"Uh-oh," Mama said. "The Birmingham News said it wasn't supposed to rain today."

"Probably just a quick summer shower. Too late to turn back now; we're almost there. We can wait it out under the shelter," Daddy said.

A stiff breeze suddenly whipped the treetops. Swaying branches sifted brown pine needles over the dirt trail.

Drip.

Drop.

Drip.

"Here it comes!" Granddaddy said.

The kids ran on ahead, and the grownups picked up their pace. Rocky and Jeff reached the top of the hill first. A stone wall, more handiwork of the Civilian Conservation Corps, bordered the overlook at shelter number two—an A-framed pavilion on stout wooden posts with log benches on facing sides. Rain pitter-pattered the cedar-shake roof. All nine of us scrunched together along the wide benches.

"So, how's work going, Rocky?" Granddaddy asked.

"Fine," Rocky said.

"Anything interesting happening down at the DeKalb County Courthouse?" he prodded.

"Yes, sir. I got to watch a court case this week where the lawyer moved the Alabama state line."

~

Our Daddy had practiced law in Fort Payne since 1950. Earlier that week, Rocky said that Daddy had called the probate office where he worked. He told him to go upstairs to the balcony of the courtroom and watch the trial going on because one of the last of the "rough and tumble" lawyers of our town was about to move the state line.

The attorney's client was charged with moonshining at the north end of DeKalb County in an area called the Big Woods. The state line between Alabama and Georgia ran somewhere down the middle of that tangled thicket of bootlegging, moonshining, car-chopping, and other illegal shenanigans. But folks just never could quite agree on exactly where that line sat. If Georgia revenuers caught a moonshiner, he'd claim that his whisky still was in Alabama *not* Georgia. If an Alabama revenuer made the arrest, the rascal would argue that his still sat on the Georgia side of the line.

Rocky described the old lawyer calling eye-witnesses to the stand who testified that they were absolutely certain that the moonshine still in question was in the State of *Georgia*. When he asked the revenuers if they were absolutely positive that the still was in Alabama, all they could say was, "Well, we're pretty sure." Needless to say, that tough-as-a-pine-knot attorney won the case, and the state line moved that day.

~

Granddaddy thought Rocky's story was a hoot and slapped his knee. Grandmama wrinkled her nose and shook her head. "Now, Mark," she said, "tell me that

143

riddle again—the one Freddy told you about the chest of drawers up in the attic."

In one month's time, the "sacred" Eberhart secret had become a popular conversation piece amongst the neighborhood families, as well as, the Nances, and the Igous.

"He said that the really rich, old lady said, 'Its beauty goes beyond the seen, and you must search for the unseen beauty,'" Mark said.

Grandmama pointed her finger. "You know what?" she said. "That sounds a lot like a Bible verse I know."

Mark's face lit up. "Really? What verse? What does it say?"

"Second Corinthians 4:18: *While we look not at the things which are seen, but at the things which are not seen; for the things which are seen are temporal; but the things which are not seen are eternal.*"

REFLECTIONS

A POINT TO PONDER

In a court of law, a witness must promise to tell the truth the whole truth and nothing but the truth. Is truth important to God?

A PEARL FROM GOD

"For the law was given through Moses; grace and truth came through Jesus Christ." (John 1:17 NIV) "Jesus told him, 'I am the way, the truth, and the life. No one can come to the Father except through Me.'" (John 14:6 NLT)

A PRINCIPLE TO LIVE BY

God's word, the Bible, is the unchanging measuring-stick for truth. Learn God's truth. Speak God's truth. Live by God's truth. *"Then you will know the truth, and the truth will set you free." (John 8:32)*

Chapter 16:

Forever and Ever Things

"...for the things which are seen are temporal; but the things which are not seen are eternal."

(2 Corinthians 4:18 KJV)

Sunday afternoon, I sat beside Mark in the treehouse with my white-leather King James Bible (ordered with plaid stamps) in my lap and Mama's thick Webster's Dictionary on the bench between us.

~

Before leaving the park, Grandmama had jotted 2 Corinthians 4:18 on a slip of paper and explained, "Mark, when you look up a verse, if you'll read it in context—that means read the verses before and after—it'll help you understand it better. Second Corinthians is the second letter the Apostle Paul wrote to fellow Christians in Corinth, Greece. Back in Paul's day, people suffered terribly for believing and sharing Jesus's Good News. So, he wrote his friends a letter, encouraging them to not give up. He told them to focus on God's everlasting promises instead of their temporary troubles."

~

Rip barked below us and chased a squirrel up the oak tree that Daddy called "Jill's tree."

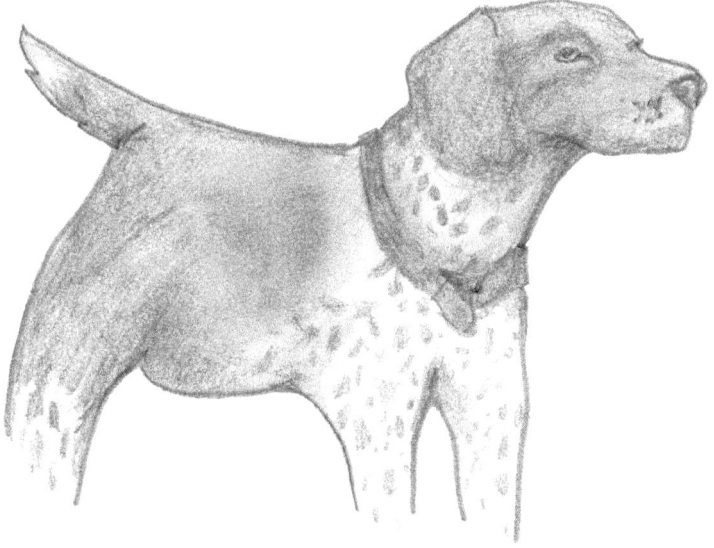

"Remember when I taught you to climb that tree?" Mark asked.

"Yep," I said.

~

Because I was too short at four years old to reach the bottom branch, Mark had picked me up and said, "Grab hold of this limb with both hands and put your feet on the trunk. Good. Now, walk up the tree and swing your leg over the limb. Okay, now, pull up and reach for the next limb. That's it. Now, keep climbing."

Minutes later, he ran inside and hollered, "Mama, come see where Jill is." She about had a heart attack when she looked out the back door and found me near the top of a tall oak, perched on a limb like a squirrel.

~

Mark picked up my Bible, unzipped the cover, and hunted for the index page. "Books of the Old Testament and New Testament," he read aloud. "Second Corinthians is..." He ran his finger down the column. "In the New Testament, right after First Corinthians—that makes sense."

He read me all of chapter four. "This is really hard to understand," he said and started back at verse one.

"You gonna read the whole thing *again*?" I asked.

"Yeah, but this time, let's write down the parts that sound important." With a yellow number-two pencil, he printed phrases in a spiral notebook and underlined the words that might link to the chest of drawers:

1. If our gospel be <u>hid</u>, it is hid to them that are <u>lost</u>.
2. But we have this <u>treasure</u> in earthen vessels.
3. We look not at the <u>things which are seen</u>.
4. For the things <u>seen</u> are <u>temporal</u>.
5. The things which are <u>not seen</u> are <u>eternal</u>.

"Okay, Jill, look up the word *temporal*."

"How do you spell it?" I asked.

"Look it up and see."

I frowned. "You sound just like Mama. How can I look up a word I can't spell?"

"Sound it out," Mark encouraged.

"T-t-t-temporal," I said and flipped past the Qs, Rs, and Ss to the Ts. "Here."

Mark took the dictionary and searched the page.

"Template...temple...tempo...temporal. Here it is. It means: *for a while, endure for a season, or temporary*." Flipping back to the *Es*, he said, "And *eternal*, means: *having infinite duration, everlasting, or forever*.

He rested his chin on his hand and thought.

And thought.

And thought.

"So, if 'seen things' are temporary and 'unseen things' are eternal, could the 'unseen beauty' of the chest of drawers be something that lasts forever and ever?"

I shrugged. "I don't know."

Mark closed Mr. Webster. "We gotta get another good look at that chest in Grandmother Eberhart's attic."

REFLECTIONS

A POINT TO PONDER

In the book of Second Corinthians, what did the Apostle Paul encourage his friends to focus on?

A PEARL FROM GOD

"Faith shows the reality of what we hope for; it is the evidence of things we cannot see." (Hebrews 11:1 NLT)
"For we live by faith, not by sight." (2 Corinthians 5:7 NIV)

A PRINCIPLE TO LIVE BY

Faith is complete trust or confidence in someone or something. Faith in Jesus Christ is not blind; it's built upon evidence—facts, eye witnesses, historical records, and personal experiences. Put your faith, trust, and confidence in God—the Father, Jesus, and the Holy Spirit—who gives strength for today and bright hope for tomorrow.

Chapter 17:

Cliff Dwellers

"How lovely is your dwelling place, O LORD of Heaven's Armies." (Psalm 84:1 NLT)

Monday morning, Freddy, Steve, Mark, and I squatted beside the red-clay bank at the corner in the neighborhood. Mark described the ancient cliff dwellers of Colorado that he'd read about in the World Book Encyclopedia as we built our own Mesa Verde.

"Mesa Verde means 'green table' in Spanish," he explained. "The cliff dwellers farmed on the flat tops of the mountains and built pueblos under the cliffs. I reckon that's why they were called Pueblo people."

Freddy used a rock to press a winding staircase into the soft clay. I picked up a stick, dug out a doorway and windows in a little, dirt hut, and then laid a line of tiny pebbles for a walkway.

"What's a pueblo?" I asked.

"An adobe house," Mark said.

"What's...."

"A house made of sun-dried clay," he answered before I finished the question.

"The Pueblo people built more than little, clay houses," Freddy said. "I saw a picture of the Cliff Palace in our encyclopedia. It had 150 rooms!"

"Like the DeKalb Hotel," Steve said.

"Hey, Mark, tell 'em 'bout Grandmama's Bible verse," I said.

"What verse?" Steve asked.

"Saturday, we were at DeSota Park for Rocky's birthday, and a thunderstorm came up while we were hiking a trail," Mark said.

"Yeah, we had to run to shelter number two to keep from gettin' soaked," I said. "Did y'all know that Mr.

Evans, the park manager, was a CCC boy and helped build all the rock walls and stuff in the park?"

"Nope," Steve said.

"Well, anyway," Mark said, "while we were waiting for the shower to pass, Grandmama said the riddle about the chest of drawers sounds like a Bible verse she knows."

"What's it say?" Freddy asked.

"Something like, don't look at things you can see; look at things you can't see," Mark said.

"That doesn't make any sense," Steve said. "How can you look at something you can't see?"

"You forgot to tell 'em the temper and turtle part," I said.

Mark laughed. "She means the temporal and eternal. The verse says that the things you can see are temporal or temporary, but the things you can't see are eternal—that means they last forever. So, I got to thinkin'. Maybe the 'unseen beauty' of the chest of

155

drawers is something we can't see that will last forever and ever."

Steve shook his head. "This chest-of-drawers thing just gets stranger and stranger." He broke a twig into tiny pieces and stacked them by a small doorway.

"What are those for?" I asked as I dropped lavender, star-shaped flowers picked from Freddy and Steve's yard all around the clay village.

"That's a woodpile for the fireplace," Steve said. "Oops, I forgot to make a chimney."

"So, what things last forever and ever?" I asked.

"God?" Steve said.

Freddy snickered. "I don't think God lives in that old chest of drawers."

"I know. Angels!" I shouted. "Me and Mary really did hear a harp or somethin' that day."

"Angels don't live in a chest of drawers either," Mark said. "Besides, I think you just heard Freddy pluckin' that old guitar. Hey, Freddy, can we go up in the attic again today?"

"Nobody's home today. They went to Chattanooga to see a cousin or somebody," Steve said.

"I'm gettin' hot," I whined. "Y'all wanna go play in the sprinkler?"

"You know we can't run a sprinkler; the well would go dry," Mark said. "Besides, we don't even have one."

"I sure hope we get city water soon," I moaned.

REFLECTIONS

A POINT TO PONDER

Freddy said that God doesn't live in a chest of drawers. Where does God live?

A PEARL FROM GOD

"Don't you realize that your body is the temple of the Holy Spirit, who lives is in you and was given to you by God? You do not belong to yourself, for God bought you with a high price. So, you must honor God with your body." (1 Corinthians 6:19-20 NLT)

A PRINCIPLE TO LIVE BY

God made our bodies, and His Spirit lives in those who believe in Him through faith in His Son, Jesus. Therefore, honor God in your body. Honor Him in your thoughts, your words, and your deeds. Honor God in the places you go, the people you go with, the things you watch, and the things you listen to.

Chapter 18:

Figurin'

"O LORD, what great works You do! And how deep are Your thoughts." (Psalm 92:5 NLT)

"The Great Houdini could get police handcuffs off his wrist merely by tapping them in the right place," Mama read at bedtime from "Houdini the Handcuff King" by Francis Sill Wickware in the *Reader's Digest: Treasury for Young Readers*.

Mark and I sat on either side of Mama on the edge of my bed.

"One of his most baffling tricks on the stage was his feat of walking through a brick wall. The trick was performed so cleverly that not even his rival magicians could guess how it was done. Houdini's secrets will not remain secret forever. On April 6, 1974..."

"Hey that's my birthday," I cried. "How old will I be by then?"

Mark did the math in his head. "Eighteen," he said. "And I'll be twenty and a half and Rocky'll be almost twenty-five and Mama will be…"

"I don't even want to think about it," she interrupted. "It'll be here before you know it. Time just flies! Let's keep reading. O*n April 6, 1974, a lawyer in New York City will open a bulky envelope which has lain sealed for more than thirty years. In it are fifty pages of Houdini's own handwriting, explaining how he managed his amazing escapes. Houdini wrote down his secrets before he died but said they were not to be opened until the hundredth anniversary of his birth.*"

"So, Houdini had *my* birthday," I said proudly.

"No, he was born first. So, you have *his* birthday," Mark said. "Go on, Mama."

"Then we will learn the answer to a question that has puzzled the world for a long time: How did Houdini do it?"

"I wonder how he did do all those tricks," Mark said thoughtfully.

Mama closed the book. "Well, I guess we'll just have to wait eleven more years to find out. Okay, let's say our prayers. It's time to go to sleep."

After the bedtime prayer, Mama kissed us and said, "Good night, sugars. Sweet dreams. I love you, both. Mark, go get in your bed, now."

"Mama?" Mark said.

"Yes."

"What things last forever?" Mark asked.

"Umm. Let me think. God. Love. People," she said. "Those are some things that last forever."

"People? People don't last forever. They die," I argued.

"Well, the body will die, but the soul and spirit will live forever," Mama said. "The Bible says that God has given us *eternal* life, and this life is in His Son, Jesus. Why do you ask?"

"Remember that verse Grandmama told us about the things seen are temporary and the things unseen are eternal?" Mark said.

"I remember."

"Well, I got to figurin'. Maybe the 'unseen beauty' of the chest of drawers is something we can't see that lasts forever."

"That's some mighty deep figuring," Mama said. "It's a mystery, all right. Now, get some sleep. You can think about it more tomorrow."

Mark started down the hall.

"Mark," Mama called, "maybe this will help. Think of temporal things as earthly and eternal things as heavenly. G'night, sugar."

REFLECTIONS

A POINT TO PONDER

What were Mark's thoughts about the chest of drawers?

A PEARL FROM GOD

"Seek the LORD while you can find Him. Call on Him while He is near. 'My thoughts are nothing like your thoughts,' says the LORD. 'And My ways are far beyond anything you could imagine. For just as the heavens are higher than the earth, so My ways are higher than your ways and My thoughts higher than your thoughts." (Isaiah 55:6,8-9 NLT)

A PRINCIPLE TO STAND ON

As you walk through daily life, seek God's thoughts on your situations and circumstances. His thoughts and ways are always higher than ours.

Chapter 19:

Uncle Frank's Clubhouse

"Don't be afraid, for I am with you. Don't be discouraged, for I am your God. I will strengthen you and help you. I will hold you up with My victorious right hand." (Isaiah 41:10 NLT)

"Freddy's going to a friend's house today, and Steve doesn't have anything to do. Can me and Steve go down to Grandmama Nance's house?" Mark asked.

"*May Steve* and *I* go to Grandmama's house," Mama corrected.

"Mama, you wanna go down to Grandmama's house with Steve?" I said. "Well, I wanna go, too!"

Mama and Mark died laughing. "No, sugar, I was just correcting your brother. You're supposed to say, '*May I*' not '*Can I*,' and you always put the other person's name before yourself," she said. "I'll go call Grandmama and ask if you can come."

Mark grinned. "Ask if we *may* come," he said.

~

Granddaddy and Grandmama Nance had built their house on Forest Avenue in the 1930s when Daddy was just a boy. A separate single-car garage with an attic sat behind the house in the shady backyard, and Granddaddy's hand-built worm bed stood beside the garage.

Granddaddy loved fishing, and Granddaddy loved taking us grandkids fishing at his farm on top of Lookout Mountain where Uncle Frank, Aunt Jo, and baby Vicki lived. Catalpa trees grew beside the dirt road leading to the ponds in the back pasture. In the late spring, Granddaddy would pick catalpa worms from the large, green leaves. "Some fish like earthworms and some like these catalpas," he'd say.

In the summertime, he'd pull the truck up to the barn and cut a juicy, red-ripe melon from the big garden that he and Frank planted every spring. We'd eat watermelon while we fished, and if someone didn't catch a bass or bream or catfish that day (which rarely happened), he'd say, "You get the snowball."

~

Mark lifted the worm-bed lid. The soil smelled rich and earthy. "Here's where we get our fishin' bait," he told Steve.

I dug into the dark, brown dirt and pulled out a red wiggler. "The bream love these, and I can bait my own hook," I bragged.

"But she can't take a fish *off* the hook. Me or Granddaddy have to do that," Mark said.

I started to stick out my tongue but stopped myself again. "Well, those fins hurt, and, besides, Mark's really good at gettin' the hooks out."

Mark closed the lid and walked into the garage. We rummaged through the junk hugging the walls. I found an old radio and tinkered with the knobs. Steve stared at a hole the ceiling.

"What's up there?" he asked.

"All kinds of neat stuff," Mark said. "It used to be Uncle Frank's clubhouse when he was a kid like us."

"Let's go up there and see," Steve said. "Where's a ladder?"

"See those boards nailed to the studs on the wall? You have to climb up that way," Mark said, "and then reach over to the hole and pull yourself in. Follow me."

He turned a metal bucket upside down for a step-stool, then climbed up the boards. Because the opening was outset from the wall by about a foot, he reached for the hole and then disappeared into the darkness. Steve followed.

Mark called down to me, "Okay, Jill, stand on the bucket. Good. Now, climb up the boards on the wall."

I held onto to the makeshift ladder with one hand and tried to grab the opening with the other. "I can't reach it," I said.

Mark laid down. "Steve, hold my legs. I'll put her up."

He gripped my wrist and yanked. I dangled from the ceiling by one arm like a chandelier and squealed like a stuck pig. Mark grabbed the other wrist. My flailing legs knocked a shovel off the wall. It hit the bucket.

CLINK!

BANG!

CLANK!

"Be still! I've got you," he yelled and hauled me into the attic.

My belly and knees scrapped across the rough boards. I started bawling. He put an arm around my shoulders. "It's okay, Jill. You're alright."

When I was done crying, we poked around the stuffy clubhouse. Mark found a stack of Royster Fertilizer books (pocket-sized memo booklets for farmers left over from the days Granddaddy worked for the Royster Fertilizer Company during the Depression). He studied the measurement tables, maps, calendar, and blank pages for notes.

"Look at these," he said. "I'm gonna ask Granddaddy if I can take one home."

Steve found a Boy Scout Handbook. I stirred through a Whitman Candy box of trinkets—skeleton keys, Orange Crush bottle caps, a whistle, two pocket knives, and a can opener.

Sweat trickled down the sides of Mark's face. "It's pretty hot up here. Let's get down. I'll go first."

Tears flooded my eyes all over again. "No!" I cried. "I'm scared. I can't reach the wall from here. I'll fall."

"Don't be scared. I'll help you," Mark said.

Nothing he said could turn my stubborn, frightened mind. Every time he started down, I started squalling.

"Steve, you get down, and go get Grandmama," Mark said.

Steve shook his head. His shyness and my fear refused to budge. So, we spent the rest of the afternoon in the clubhouse oven. I reckon we would have stayed up there till the cows came home if Uncle Frank hadn't finally pulled up the driveway in his brown station wagon. Mark stuck his head through the hole and hollered, "Up here!"

Frank climbed the rungs on the wall. With one muscular arm, he swung me from the attic and toted me down.

REFLECTIONS

A POINT TO PONDER

Why would Steve not go for help? Why wouldn't I let Mark help me down?

A PEARL FROM GOD

"This is My command—be strong and courageous! Do not be afraid or discouraged. For the LORD your God is with you wherever you go." (Joshua 1:9 NLT)

A PRINCIPLE TO LIVE BY

When you feel shy or afraid, remember that God is always with you. Ask Him to help you and to give you courage.

Chapter 20:

Keep Looking

"...Keep on seeking, and you will find..."

(Matthew 7:7 NLT)

Steve, Mark, and I sat around the table in the breakfast room gulping orange juice and devouring corn curls and rice crispy treats. Grandmama mopped my face with a cool, wet rag. "Why didn't y'all come get me?" she asked.

"She cried every time I tried," Mark said, "and Steve didn't wanna go in by himself."

Steve grinned and stuffed a gooey puffed-rice square into his mouth.

"I was scared," I said. "Mark 'bout killed me getting me up there."

"No, I didn't," Mark said. "I had you all the time."

"Well, next time Mark, come get help even if she cries."

"Yes, ma'am," he said.

"Steve, did Mark and Jill tell you my mother's story about the chest of drawers in your grandmother's attic?" Grandmama said.

"Yes, ma'am," Steve said.

"Grandmama," Mark said, "I've been thinking about that verse you gave us—the temporary and the eternal one—and I was wondering, besides God and angels and love and people, what are some other things that last forever?"

"Well, First Corinthians 13:13 says, in addition to love, that faith and hope will last forever, and Isaiah 40:8 says the word of God stands forever."

"So, God, angels, people, faith, hope, love, and the word of God," Mark said. "Anything else?"

"Let me think. Psalm 111:10 says praise to God endures forever."

"Grandmama, how come you know so much about the Bible?" I asked.

"Because I've been reading it and studying it and teaching it in Sunday School for a long, long time. See this little pin on my smock?" She pointed to a six-sided, gold frame around a tiny golden cross with the initials WSCS.

"Yes, ma'am," I said.

Grandmama unfastened the clasp and pinned it to my T-shirt. "This is my Women's Society Christian Service pin, and I want you to have it. Maybe you can pass it down to your granddaughter one day. And when you get a little older, I want you to have the rocking chair in the back bedroom that my grandpapa, Columbus Washington Robison, made when he came home from the Civil War in 1865. Grandmaw rocked her seven babies in it, and maybe you can rock your babies in it one day."

I studied the little pin on my shirt. "Thank you, Grandmama."

"How come she gets all the good stuff?" Mark asked.

Grandmama patted his hand. "Oh, don't you worry, Mark. I have things set aside for you and Rocky and Vicki, too."

Cheese dust from the corn curls covered Mark's fingers. He wiped them on his shorts. "Grandmama, what could God or angels or people or love or faith or hope or the Bible or praise have to do with a chest of drawers?" he asked.

"I don't know, sugar. Just keep looking."

REFLECTIONS

A POINT TO PONDER

What three things listed in 1 Corinthians 13:13 last forever?

A PEARL FROM GOD

"Three things will last forever—faith, hope, and love— and the greatest of these is love." (1 Corinthians 13:13 NLT) "And you must love the LORD your God with all your heart, all your soul, and all your strength. The second is equally important: 'Love your neighbor as yourself." No other commandments are greater than these." (Mark 12:30-31 NLT)

A PRINCIPLE TO LIVE BY

Love God everyday by obeying Him and honoring Him. Love others everyday with kindness and compassion even when they act unlovable.

Chapter 21:

Mark's Plan

"I can do all things through Christ which strengthens me." (Philippians 4:13 NASB)

During the children's minute in the worship service the following Sunday, Mrs. Brown read, *"Be careful for nothing; but in every thing by prayer and supplication with thanksgiving let your requests be made known unto God. And the peace of God, which passeth all understanding, shall keep your hearts and minds through Christ Jesus.* Philippians chapter four, verses six and seven. And skipping down to verse thirteen, *I can do all things through Christ which strengtheneth me."*

"Boys and girls, did you know that Philippians is a letter written by the Apostle Paul to the first church founded in Europe?" Mrs. Brown said.

I watched Mark's hand shoot up.

"Yes, Mark?" she said.

"He wrote a letter to Christians in Corinth, Greece, too." he said proudly.

"You are absolutely correct, Mark. Paul actually wrote *thirteen* letters, which are books of the New Testament. In his letter to the church in Philippi, he encouraged believers to be joyful in the midst of their problems. He taught that the secret to joy and contentment is: we can do all things—even hard or painful things—through Jesus Christ who gives us strength."

Mark's face brightened. He leaned over and whispered in my ear, "I gotta plan."

~

Monday morning, we pedaled our bicycles up the chert road to house number two in the neighborhood and found Freddy wrapped in an US Army hammock strung between two hickory trees.

"Get on the other side, Mark," Steve called.

Mark dropped his bike to the ground and grabbed the other end of the hammock. He and Steve swung Freddy—not back and forth like a swing, but around and around and around like a jump rope.

"I wanna ride," I cried.

After we each took a turn in the canvas Ferris wheel, we ran to house number one and climbed into the attic. Freddy, Steve, Mark, and I stared at the chest of drawers.

Mark said, "Hey, do y'all remember that verse Mrs. Brown read to the kids yesterday?"

"The one about we can do anything when Jesus helps us?" Freddy said.

"Yeah, that's the one. Well, I gotta plan. Maybe nobody ever asked Jesus to help 'em find the unseen beauty. So, let's ask Him," Mark said.

"You mean pray?" Steve said.

"Yeah, let's pray and ask God for help," Mark said.

Steve folded his hands. "Okay, Mark, you pray."

"Uh, Freddy's the oldest. You pray, Freddy," Mark said.

"It was your idea," Freddy said. "You pray, Mark."

"I'll pray," I said and folded my hands and closed my eyes. "Dear Lord, please help us find the unseen beauty. Amen."

Steve opened one eye. "That's all you're gonna say? Brother Warlick says a lot of Thees and Thous when he prays."

"Well, I said, 'please help us find *THE* unseen beauty.'"

"Now, what do we do?" Freddy asked.

"I don't know," Mark said.

I touched a tarnished knight. "Grandmaw sure needs to polish these soldiers again and make 'em shiny. They're all green."

Mark picked up a rag hanging over a picture frame and rubbed the knight on the right-hand side. It twisted.

TING!

"Did y'all hear that?" I cried. "I told you I heard something the other day."

Mark turned the knight again.

TING!

DING!

"Music!" Freddy exclaimed. "Let me try."

Freddy turned the knight halfway around.

TING!

DING!

CHING!

He wound it around and around and around again. When he let go, a pure melody chimed from deep within the old chest.

"It's a music box!" Freddy shouted.

REFLECTIONS

A POINT TO PONDER

What was Mark's plan?

A PEARL FROM GOD

"And we are confident that [God] hears us whenever we ask for anything that pleases Him. And since we know He hears us when we make our requests, we also know He will give us what we ask for." (1 John 5:14-15 NLT) "Yet you don't have what you want because you don't ask God for it." (James 4:2b NLT)

A PRINCIPLE TO LIVE BY

Pray. Always ask God for His help and trust His answer— even when He says wait or no.

Chapter 22:

Talk of the Town

"I'll make you famous for generations; you'll be the talk of the town for a long, long time."

(Psalm 45:17 The Message)

Steve cried, "Music *was* a clue!"

"I've heard that song before," Mark said eagerly. "Mrs. White plays it on the organ at church. It's a hymn, and hymns are *beautiful* praises to God, and the Bible says that *praise* to God lasts forever! *Music* is the 'unseen beauty.' Let's go tell your grandmother."

We scrambled down the ladder and flew to the kitchen where Grandmother Eberhart was stirring a pot of homemade vegetable soup. Freddy, Steve, Mark, and I all talked at the same time.

"It plays music!"

"We found the unseen beauty!"

"You gotta come see!"

"We asked Jesus to help us, and He did!"

"Calm down, children, calm down," Grandmother Eberhart said. "Now, what happened? One at a time. You go first, Mark."

"We prayed and asked Jesus to help us find the unseen beauty, and I picked up a rag to polish the knights on top of the chest 'cause their all green, and one turned, and we heard a dingin' sound, and Freddy twisted it around and around, and the chest of drawers played a hymn from church!" Mark said.

"The old chest of drawers is a *music box*!" Freddy cried.

Grandmother Eberhart shook her head. "Well, I declare," she said. "After all these years. I'm so proud of you children. I never, in all my born days, heard of a chest of drawers playing music. It must be very rare."

"And probably worth a *whole* bunch of money, too!" Freddy said.

"Well, you know, Freddy, that old chest of drawers really belongs to the city of Fort Payne, not the Eberharts. Our family just served as its keeper for all these years. We need to let somebody in town know what you've found. I'll call your mama at the City Hall."

~

Freddy and Steve's mother worked as the bookkeeper for the Fort Payne Water Department located in the City Hall building on Gault Avenue. When we visited her office with Freddy and Steve, she always let us kids eat sugar cubes from the bowl beside the coffee pot. I liked visiting Mrs. Eberhart.

~

Mrs. Eberhart promised to contact Mayor Purdy immediately about our discovery, and by the next day, the old chest of drawers was the talk of the town.

"It's a music box," Mrs. Abbott told Mrs. Fischer.

"The old chest plays a hymn," Mrs. Fischer told Mrs. Killian.

"It used to be in the DeKalb Hotel," Mrs. Killian told Mrs. Pate.

"And it's been in the Eberhart's attic for years and years," Mrs. Pate told Mrs. Stout.

"The children figured out the secret," Mrs. Stout told Mrs. Ingram.

"They say it's very valuable," Mrs. Ingram told Mrs. Kuykendall.

"It came all the way from Germany," Mrs. Kuykendall told Mrs. Mince.

"Mayor Purdy put a call into the Smithsonian Institute," Mrs. Mince told Mrs. Wear.

"A crew of men are moving the chest from the Eberhart's attic to City Hall, today," Mrs. Wear told Mrs. Martin.

REFLECTIONS

A POINT TO PONDER

What was the unseen beauty of the chest of drawers?

A PEARL FROM GOD

"Praise the LORD! Praise God in His sanctuary; praise Him in His mighty heaven! Praise Him for His mighty works; praise His unequaled greatness! Praise Him with a blast of the ram's horn; praise Him with the lyre and harp! Praise Him with the tambourine and dancing; praise Him with strings and flutes! Praise Him with a clash of cymbals; praise Him with loud clanging cymbals. Let everything that breathes sing praise to the LORD! Praise the LORD!" (Psalm 150 NLT)

A PRINCIPLE TO LIVE BY

Praise is the heart-felt expression of approval and admiration of someone or something. God deserves our praise above all people, places, or things. Today, express your admiration and gratitude to God the Father, Son, and Holy Spirit.

Chapter 23:

Composer of Praise

"And they sang...the song of the Lamb, saying, 'Great and marvelous are Your works, O Lord God, the Almighty; righteous and true are Your ways, King of the nations!'" (Revelation 15:3 NLT)

Two weeks later, an entourage of specialists from the American History Museum and American Art Museum of the Smithsonian Institute (a collection of museums and research centers run by the U.S. government and founded "for the increase and diffusion of knowledge" in 1846 in Washington D.C.) paraded into the City Hall of Fort Payne, Alabama. Mayor Purdy greeted the men and women with a broad smile and a firm handshake. Rogers Culpepper snapped a photo, and Ben Smith, the new editor for the Times Journal, scribbled notes on a pad of paper. Freddy, Steve, Mark, and I, dressed in our Sunday best, stood beside the cleaned and polished chest of drawers.

With pomp and flair, Freddy retold the story of the chest of drawers from its Boom Days to Grandmother Eberhart's attic. Mark added Grandmaw Robison's memories.

"So, the chest of drawers originated from Germany?" Dr. Barnett, an older gentleman with gray hair and a mustache, said.

"Yes, sir," Mark answered. "Grandmaw said somebody famous who liked music had owned it."

"Interesting," he remarked and made a note on his pad of paper. "Steve, will you do the honors and demonstrate how the chest works, please?"

"Me?" Steve said. "Uh, yes, sir."

Steve wound the right-hand knight on horseback, now shiny as a new dime. The old chest of drawers chimed the beautiful melody. A dark-haired lady in glasses shaped like cat eyes closed her eyes and swayed to the music.

"That song is 'For the Beauty of the Earth.' It's a hymn," I piped.

"Very good," the cat-eye lady said.

"Children, I'd like for you to meet Dr. Elizabeth Schmidt from Julliard School of Performing Arts in New York City. Our team invited her to join us because of her expertise in hymnology," Dr. Barnett explained.

Dr. Schmidt turned toward Dr. Barnett. "The lyrics of this praise hymn were written by Folliott Sandford Pierpont of England; however, the melody of the song was composed by Conrad Kocher, an 1800s organist and choirmaster in the Stiftskirche or

Collegiate Church in Stuttgart, Germany," she explained. "He founded the School for Sacred Song in Stuttgart and popularized four-part harmony. Do you suppose Kocher himself was the original owner of this magnificent work of art?"

"If he truly was the original owner," Dr. Barnett said, "we've made quite an unprecedented discovery."

"Hey, wait a minute, mister. *You* didn't make a pressed-and-dented discovery. You didn't find the chest of drawers *or* the secret. *We* did," I cried, then slapped my hand over my mouth. "Oops! Sorry, sir."

Dr. Barnett pressed his lips together to smother a laugh.

Freddy stepped up and put a hand on my shoulder. "Yes, sir, she's right. The four of us friends from the neighborhood, we found the chest in Grandmother's attic and the hidden music box. Jill heard the music first."

I smiled up at Freddy. Four friends from the neighborhood. I was finally one of the gang.

"I beg your pardon, young lady and gentlemen. You are absolutely correct," Dr. Barnett said.

Dr. Schmidt, the cat-eye lady, asked, "Children, why do you suppose Mrs. Higgins described the chest of drawers as having unseen beauty?"

"Well, the music box was hidden, so that makes it unseen," Mark said. "And it plays a hymn of praise to God, and praise is beautiful and will last forever."

Dr. Schmidt nodded enthusiastically. "Very good, children. Very good, indeed. Dr. Barnett, I have connections at the State University of Music and Performing Arts in Stuttgart. It's one of the oldest schools of its kind. Perhaps Dr. Klein, the head master, can shed some light on the genesis of this mystery."

Dr. Barnett nodded. "Very well," he said. "Mayor Purdy, thank you for contacting us. We'll notify you when the investigation is completed. Good day, sir."

REFLECTIONS

A POINT TO PONDER

How did I feel when Freddy called us "four friends" from the neighborhood?

A PEARL FROM GOD

"Never let loyalty and kindness leave you! Tie them around your neck as a reminder. Write them deep within your heart. Then you will find favor with both God and people, and you will earn a good reputation." *(Proverbs 3:3-4 NLT)*

A PRINCIPLE TO LIVE BY

Remember that loyalty (faithful devotion) and kindness are the pathway to friendship. Walk in loyalty and kindness day after day after day.

Chapter 24:

Copper Pancakes

"Give, and you will receive. Your gift will return to you in full—pressed down, shaken together to make room for more, running over, and poured into your lap."

(Luke 6:38 NLT)

Mayor Purdy declared the area surrounding the old chest off-limits and secured it behind red velvet ropes between brass posts. For weeks, a steady stream of curious onlookers visited City Hall. Grandmaw Robison stood first in line.

~

Summertime ended.

~

Labor Day passed.

~

Musical-chest chitter-chatter faded to a whisper.

~

School began again.

~

Freddy and Mark were assigned to Mrs. Wilson's fifth-grade class at Forest Avenue Elementary School. Steve was a fourth grader in Miss Deware's class. Mary was in Miss Crowley's second-grade class, and I was in the other second-grade classroom taught by Mrs. Igou (a relative of Dr. Igou). Three days a week, Mama was the new Forest Avenue Elementary School librarian. Paul Hamilton, our principal, had recruited her over the summer.

One afternoon after school, Mama turned left on Gault Avenue instead of heading up the mountain.

"Where we goin'?" I asked.

"To the train depot. Your daddy told me at lunch that an old steam engine is passing through Fort Payne at 3:30 this afternoon, and he thought you'd like to see it."

"Can we put pennies on the tracks?" Mark asked.

A puzzled look crossed my face. "Why would we put pennies on the tracks?"

"The train will smash 'em as flat as pancakes, and we can keep 'em as souvenirs," Mark said.

At 3:15, Mama parked the Ford facing the tracks in front of the depot. The Fort Payne Depot (a fancy building of locally-quarried pink and white sandstone with a castle-like tower and an arched doorway) had been built toward the end of the Boom Days in 1891. It stood across the street from Union Park and served the Great Southern Railroad.

Mama dug into her coin purse for change. "Here's two pennies each," she said.

Mark and I hopped from the car and ran to the tracks. We lined four pennies along the steel rails.

"Hey, Mark."

We turned around. A boy from Mark's class stood right behind us. Both hands were buried in the pockets of his dark-blue jeans and the toes of his red high-top basketball shoes rubbed together in a nervous sort of way.

"Hey, Anthony. You waitin' for the steam engine, too?" Mark asked.

"Yep."

Mama called through the open window, "Come get in the car, and we'll read a story while we wait for the train."

"Can Anthony come, too?" Mark asked.

"Of course," Mama answered. "Hi, Anthony.'

He waved.

"Wanna wait with us?" Mark said.

Anthony's lips curved to a lop-sided grin. "Sure."

Mama opened the *Reader's Digest: Treasury for Young Readers* to "The City that Died to Live" by Donald and Louise Peattie:

"The city of Pompeii basked among its silvery olive groves and dark umbrella pines. No one looked anxiously at Mount Vesuvius, five miles away, for peaceful vineyards clothed the old volcano's sides and its silent crater was plugged with rock. Suddenly an earthquake shook the city. With the first shock of the earthquake, the everyday life of Pompeii was at an end forever. The volcano poured forth a weird cloud whose top spread out and out..."

WOO-A-WOO!

WOO-A-WOOOOOOO!

"Here it comes!" Mark shouted and pointed south toward Collinsville.

We piled out of the car and joined other children and parents gathered in front of the depot.

The clickety-clack, clickety-clack of wheels on the rails echoed up the valley. Puffs of dark smoke smudged the clear, blue sky. When the train came into view, the engineer blew the whistle again and waved at the crowd.

I counted the cars as they passed. "One, two, three, four…"

After the red caboose was well on its way toward Valley Head, we hurried to the tracks and searched for the pennies.

"Here's one," I squealed and held up a flat copper disk.

"Here's two more," Mark shouted.

"And there's the last one," I said and pointed to a shiny object in the gravel between the rails.

Anthony watched in silence as we admired our treasures.

I stretched out my hand. "Here, Anthony," I said. "You can have one of mine."

He grinned and took the copper pancake. "Thanks."

On the way home, Mama said, "That was nice of you, Jill, to give Anthony one of your pennies."

"Yeah," Mark said. "I could tell it made him happy."

It made me feel happy, too.

REFLECTIONS

A POINT TO PONDER

How did Anthony feel when I shared my souvenir? How did I feel after I shared?

A PEARL FROM GOD

"You should remember the words of the Lord Jesus: 'It is more blessed to give than to receive." (Acts 20:35 NLT)

A PRINCIPLE TO LIVE BY

Eagerly share with others. For one day, *"King [Jesus] will say, 'I tell you the truth, when you did it to one of the least of these my brothers and sisters, you were doing it to Me!'" (Matthew 25:40 NLT)*

Chapter 25:

Official Report

"They reported everything God had done through them." (Acts 15:4 NLT)

The October sun rose later and fell earlier. Splatters of crimson, gold, and pumpkin-orange painted over the green mountainside. Goldenrods and brown-eyed Susans dotted the field beside Granddaddy Eberhart's pond and waved in the breeze along the chert road of the neighborhood. Two squirrels played chase in the front window of Southern Hardware store on Gault Avenue.

Two days before Halloween, Daddy brought home an official-looking envelope from the mayor's office addressed to: Master Mark and Miss Jill Watson. An identical parcel in the Eberhart's mailbox read:

You are cordially invited

to

Mayor Fred Purdy's Office

Monday, November 4th at 4:00 PM

City Hall

Fort Payne, Alabama

~

On Monday, Freddy's eleventh birthday, Mayor Purdy welcomed both families into his office. He shook hands with Mr. Eberhart, Daddy, and Rocky, and he gave me a hug. Please, have a seat ladies and gentlemen. I wanted you to be the first to hear the Smithsonian's prodigious report.

I leaned over to Mark. "What's a pro-genius report?" I whispered.

Mark shrugged.

Mayor Purdy cleared his throat and read:

October 18, 1963

The Smithsonian Institute

10th St & Constitution Ave. NW

Washington, DC 20560

Mayor Fred Purdy

City Hall

101 Gault Ave.

Fort Payne, AL 35967

Dear Mayor Purdy,

Thank you for inviting our research team to your lovely town. I hereby submit to you the official findings of the Smithsonian Institute of the United States of America in regard to one said musical chest of drawers currently in the possession of the town of Fort Payne, Alabama.

As promised, Dr. Elizabeth Schmidt from Julliard School of Performing Arts in New York City contacted Dr. Jonas Klein at the State University of Music and Performing Arts in Stuttgart, Germany. Dr. Klein, thenceforth, contacted the Stiftskirche and learned that the church where Conrad Kocher served as choirmaster in the 1800s was heavily damaged in 1944 by bombing raids near the end of World War II. Its library, books, and handwritten records, however, were miraculously preserved. Among the archives, Dr. Klein and the church officials uncovered Conrad Kocher's own personal journal. Their findings:

- In 1838, Kocher composed a melody called DIX, which was later used to accompany lyrics written by Folliott Sandford Pierpont in 1864. The hymn of praise created was entitled "For the Beauty of the Earth."

- In 1871, the year before his death, Kocher commissioned a master carpenter, an artisan clockmaker, and a sculptor of metal to craft a one-of-a-kind chest of drawers with a hidden music box. The music box was fashioned to play the musician's DIX composition. Clockworks powered the concealed musical case that produced notes by a set of pins on a revolving cylinder plucking finely-tuned teeth of steel. One of the three hand-sculpted bronze knights on horseback served as the winding key. When Conrad Kocher died on December 3, 1872, he bequeathed the chest of drawers to his niece and only living relative, Hannah Kocher Higgins, a musician in Boston, Massachusetts.

The City of Stuttgart, Germany humbly requests that the bona fide Kocher chest of drawers be returned to the Stiftskirche Church in exchange for $100,000 plus shipping costs to be paid in full to the town of Fort Payne, Alabama.

Congratulations, Mayor Purdy! It has been our pleasure to serve you. Do not hesitate to contact us if we may be of further assistance.

Sincerely,

Bryson Barnett

Dr. Bryson J. Barnett

Curator, American History Museum

Smithsonian Institute

REFLECTIONS

A POINT TO PONDER

How did our discovery help our hometown? What would have happened if we had given up the search?

A PEARL FROM GOD

"So, do not throw away this confident trust in the Lord. Remember the great reward it brings you! Patient endurance is what you need now, so that you will continue to do God's will. Then you will receive all that He has promised." (Hebrews 10:35-36 NLT)

A PRINCIPLE TO LIVE BY

Hard work, patience, and endurance pays off. Keep working and never give up on God's assignments for you.

Chapter 26:

One Big Neighborhood

"Lord, through all the generations You have been our home! Before the mountains were born, before You gave birth to the earth and the world, from beginning to end, You are God." (Psalm 90:1-2 NLT)

I chased Frankie in the backyard while Mark, Freddy, and Steve finished the "big surprise" down in the woods. Frankie was a stray Walker Hound that had shown up skinny and hungry at house number four in the neighborhood. I'd never had my very own dog before. So, I named him and claimed him. After a couple of bowls of scraps mixed with Purina Dog Chow, Frankie decided to set up camp for a spell.

The boys strutted out of the woods, all smiles and looking as proud as peacocks. Mark pulled a bandana from a jacket pocket.

"Okay, Jill," he said, "we're gonna blindfold you and take you to the surprise."

"Will I like it?" I asked.

Steve grinned. "You're gonna love it."

Mark tied the kerchief over my eyes. "Can ya see anything?"

"Nope."

He grabbed my right hand; Freddy grabbed the left. They led me past the Tarzan swing Daddy had hung from a tree limb and down a path into the woods. I stumbled over a root.

"Careful," Mark said. "Watch your step."

I laughed. "How can I watch my step? I can't see anything."

After a short hike through crunchy leaves, Mark announced, "We're here" and untied the bandana.

"Tada!" Mark, Freddy, and Steve cried together.

I opened my eyes at the foot of Big Oak, a favorite tree that grew as tall as a church steeple and as broad as a barn door on the edge of the bluff. The limbs towered above my head, and it was hard for me to climb. Now, boards nailed to the trunk formed a crooked ladder.

Overhead, a plank floor stretched between two large branches with crude handrails on either side.

"Your very own treehouse, my lady," Freddy said.

Steve grinned. "Just like *Swiss Family Robinson*."

"Do you like it?" Mark asked eagerly.

"I love it! Thank you," I said and hugged their necks.

CLANG!

CLANG!

CLANG!

"Why's Mama's calling us in so early?" I said.

"I don't know," Mark said. "Let's go see."

Mama stood at the back door in a burnt-orange-colored jacket with a floral headscarf tied under her chin. Smoke curled from the rock chimney.

"It's pretty chilly, today," she said. "I thought you children might like some cocoa and popcorn."

"Yes, ma'am!"

In the living room, we sat crisscross-applesauce on the green rug in front of a crackling fire. Yellow and blue flames licked the split oak logs. Mama set a tray with four mugs and a wide bowl of buttery popcorn on the rock hearth. Mini marshmallows floated atop steaming chocolate. She handed me a cup.

"Careful, sugar, it's hot. Don't burn yourself, and don't spill it," she said.

"Mama, so, why do you think that rich lady left such a valuable chest of drawers in Fort Payne?" Mark asked.

"Well, they say she no longer had any close family to speak of, and she knew Fort Payne was in hard times because of the failed mines. I think she just wanted to help."

"Like a good neighbor," Freddy said.

Mama nodded. "Yes, Freddy, like a good neighbor."

"Mama, what's Mayor Purdy gonna do with all that money?" I asked.

"Well, it's a big and important decision, so he and the city council are meeting every week to figure that out. There are lots of needs around town—schools to repair and roads to patch up."

"I think they should pipe city water up the mountain to our neighborhood since we're the reason they have all that money," I said.

"Yeah," Steve said, "that sounds like a good idea."

"Hmm, I don't know. Sounds a bit selfish, don't you think?" Mama said. "Wanting the town to spend a once-in-a-lifetime blessing on ourselves? You know, I like to think of our neighborhood as just a little part of one big, beautiful neighborhood called Fort Payne, Alabama."

I nodded. "Yes, ma'am. You're right. I was just thinking of myself and not being neighborly."

Mama kissed the top of my head.

~

Days passed.

~

Friday, November 22, 1963 was a blustery, gray day. After lunch, Mrs. Igou told us kids to line up at the door because it was our turn to pick up trash on the playground.

We marched down the wooden steps and out the back door. From the sidewalk, I spotted Mark on the monkey bars and waved. Suddenly, a fifth-grade girl burst from the second story of the other building and ran down the metal stairway. She was crying. I heard her shout, "President Kennedy's been shot!"

I felt scared and wanted to run to Mark.

Back in the classroom, the intercom crackled. Mr. Hamilton's voice shook as he announced that President John F. Kennedy, the 35th President of the United States of America, had been assassinated. Our president was dead. Teachers and students cried. A sixth-grade boy lowered the American flag to half-mast.

On Sunday, my family huddled together on the couch in front of the television. We watched the horse-drawn caisson carry the flag-draped coffin to the United

States Capitol to lie in state. I saw Daddy wipe a tear from his eye.

On Monday, the day of the funeral, schools and businesses closed. The television cameras focused on the late president's wife and children. Caroline gripped her mother's hand, and little JFK Jr. saluted his father's casket.

I felt sad and laid my head on Daddy's knee. He patted my back.

~

Thanksgiving Day arrived three days later. Granddaddy, Grandmama, Aunt Dot, Uncle Frank, Aunt Jo, and baby Vicki came for dinner at house number four of the neighborhood. Granddaddy promised me a dime if I would sit still and not talk for ten minutes. It was hard, but I got the dime.

~

On Christmas Day, a light dusting of snow fell. Lookout Mountain looked like a powdered donut.

"Santa" brought a new Flexible Flyer sled with red metal runners. Rocky pulled on his new Georgia Tech sweatshirt and ran outside with Mark and me to try out the sled. The metal runners stuck in the thick, brown leaves.

~

On New Year's Eve, Mama and Daddy let me stay up till midnight for the first time ever. Rocky and Mark blew cow-horn bugles to welcome in 1964. I tore up a Birmingham newspaper and threw confetti into the air. Daddy said, "Jill, you need to clean that up."

~

On Friday, January 17, 1964 at 10:45 A.M. in the Leone Cole Auditorium of Jacksonville State College in Jacksonville, Alabama, Grandmama (Mrs. Jessilee Robison Watson Nance) waltzed across the stage and received a hard-earned second diploma: Master of Science in Education. The Reverend Billy Adams gave the invocation, and Dr. William J. Calvert, Jr. gave the baccalaureate address. For the recessional, the college band, under the direction of Mr. David Walters, played "Proud Heritage" by Latham.

~

By springtime, Fort Payne schools were repaired, roads were patched, and Rocky's birthday wish finally came true—our neighborhood stretched down a gravel road along the lower brow of Lookout Mountain had city water.

~~~

Seasons rolled into years. Rocky graduated from Auburn University and then followed Daddy's footsteps to the University of Alabama School of Law. He returned to Fort Payne in 1974, and Daddy's firm grew to Watson and Watson, Attorneys at Law.

Daddy died in 1994.

Mama died in 2003.

In 2008, Rocky and his wife, Donna, built a lovely home close to the waterfall below house number four in the old neighborhood. Today, they are the proud parents of three, and five beautiful grandgirls call them Pop and Nonny.

In 2011, Rocky's daughter, Tamara, moved back to Fort Payne with her husband, Aubrey Neeley, establishing Watson, Neeley, and Neeley, Attorneys at Law.

In 2018, Tamara's family moved into the remodeled house number four of the neighborhood. Mama and Daddy would be so happy. Their next-door neighbors in house number three are none other than our beloved, longtime friend, Steve Eberhart, and his wife, Brenda.

~

After high school, Mark went to Jacksonville State University and also served in the National Guard. He transferred to Auburn University his junior year and earned his doctorate degree from Auburn's School of Veterinary Medicine. Dr. Mark Watson has lovingly served pets and their families at the Bell County Animal Clinic in Middlesboro, Kentucky for over thirty-five years.

He and his wife, Debra, are the proud parents of two and proud grandparents-times-three.

~

I followed my Mark to Auburn University and married my high school sweetheart, Phillip Glassco, in 1977. After earning a Master of Science in Speech Pathology from the University of Southern Mississippi, I retired at the ripe old age of twenty-five to stay home with three great kids. I began writing women's Bible studies in 2004 and Christian children's books in 2011. Today, we live in Birmingham, Alabama, relishing life as Granddaddy and Memaw to seven wonderful grandkids. Mary Igou Shurett is still one of my best friends in the whole wide world.

~

As I look back across the decades to that fun summer of 1963 and the beautiful autumns, winters, springs, and summers that trailed, they pale in comparison to the everyday unseen beauty of family, friendships, faith, and love in a once-upon-a-time neighborhood atop Lookout Mountain in Fort Payne, Alabama.

For the beauty of the earth,

For the glory of the skies,

For the love which from our birth over

and around us lies;

Christ our God, to Thee we raise

This our hymn of grateful praise.

For the joy of human love, brother, sister, parent, child,

Friends on earth, and friends above,

for all gentle thoughts and mild;

Christ our God, to Thee we raise

This our hymn of grateful praise." [2]

---

[2] FOR THE BEAUTY OF THE EARTH. Lyrics: Folliott Sandford Pierpont, 1864. Melody: DIX, Conrad Kocher, 1838.

Pictures

FIGURE 1. FIRST METHODIST CHURCH CONFIRMATION CLASS 1963

FIGURE 2. TOP – JILL WATSON (GLASSCO) 1962. BOTTOM LEFT –
MARK WATSON 1963. BOTTOM RIGHT – ROCKY WATSON 1963.

FIGURE 3. LEFT – STEVE EBERTHART 1963.   RIGHT - MARY IGOU
(SHURETT) 1962.

FIGURE 4. FREDDY EBERHEART, STEVE EBERHART, AND JILL
WATSON 1962

FIGURE 5. FREDDY AND STEVE EBERHART AND JILL WATSON 1962

FIGURE 6. WINFRED AND JILL WATSON 1963

FIGURE 7. ROCKY, MARK, AND JILL WATSON 1963

FIGURE 8. VERNA, ROCKY, MARK, AND JILL WATSON AT DESOTO
STATE PARK 1959

FIGURE 9. VERNA, ROCKY, MARK, AND JILL WATSON EASTER 1960

FIGURE 10. HOMEPLACE IN THE NEIGHBORHOOD, LOOKOUT
MOUNTAIN 1960

FIGURE 11. ROCKY WATSON, JILL WATSON GLASSCO, MARK WATSON CHRISTMAS 2019.